EMPTY PALACE

A LEGEND OF THE CAROLYNGIAN AGE

JOSEPH S SAMANIEGO

Empty Palace

Written by Joseph S. Samaniego.

Published by Joseph S. Samaniego, 2023

ISBN: 978-1-7369563-6-6

Mage's Moon Publishing

Maps and Cover created by

Joseph S. Samaniego

Table of Contents

KARGILDAN

SCARS OF THE TIME BEFORE TIME

"They say some explorers found a city."

"Explorers? Let me guess, you've been reading about the Far-Off Kingdom again?" Lestrade asked.

Her friend looked excited at the name of the mythical kingdom that disappeared long ago. If it ever even existed.

"If they found it, then we could plan an expedition ourselves," replied Amasis, an unassuming scholar and mage centered at the Great Library of Cartogenia.

The pair were in a small study room off of the main corridor of the massive building used by mages and sages not affiliated with the Mage Guild.

Amasis had read every bit of scroll that wrote of the fabled land. Lestrade closed the book she'd been trying to enjoy and stood from her chair. She put the book on a nearby table, then brushed her blonde hair from in front of her eyes.

"Okay Amasis, let's think about this," she began, walking to a globe. "The Far-Off Kingdom is a story from ages long past, said to contain treasures beyond comprehension. Yet, it has never, in over several thousand years, been discovered," Lestrade pointed to the globe. "The last expedition, twenty years ago, failed when the Sile ruler was killed," she said, pointing to a spot on the globe in the northern vicinity. Lestrade smiled and spun the globe with her finger.

Amasis grinned at his friend. "Yes, the Sile ruler accompanied by an old goddess!"

"A legend by the Lotcalans to glorify their tales of war. Common for the northern tribesmen."

Amasis shook his head. "Not tribesmen, viable civilizations, but apart from that, the tales of the old gods ring true today."

"Yes, yes, fallen angels from the Creator after a great war in the heavens. Who hasn't heard this story?" Lestrade said dismissively, with a wave of her hand. "If we even care to believe in such stories of deities. I put little stock into gods."

Amasis continued to smile at his friend.

"What? Why are you smiling so much?" Lestrade asked, then she thought about it.

She knew Amasis wasn't a rube. He was the second most intelligent person she'd ever known. He was also the foremost authority on the Far-Off Kingdom legends.

Lestrade also knew he wasn't one to jump to ridiculous conclusions so easily.

"What have you found?" she asked.

"A scroll from The Age of the Red Moon!" Amasis gingerly pulled the twine rolled linen from his cloak. "It is well over four thousand years old and still intact!"

"I feel magic emanating from it," Amasis grinned. "It says that the old gods were cast down, and another war began between Ymir and Malum. Ymir's daughter Ren betrayed her father, but instead of fighting for Malum, she fought alongside Wohd. Mortals fought alongside the gods, and after generations, Ymir won. After his victory, Ymir cast Malum, Wohd, and Ren further away into an abyss created by Viri Al Sim."

"Viri Al Sim wasn't an old god. Was he?" Lestrade asked.

Amasis shrugged. "I hadn't thought so, but here whoever wrote this called him the builder of the Thin Place and the beyond," Amasis continued to read. "In the ashes of the forest that was destroyed when the children fell from the heavens, the mortals built a city to honor them."

"A link to the Far-Off Kingdom?" Lestrade asked.

"I don't know for sure, but I can't imagine another," Amasis looked up before continuing. "The city grew in magnitude of arcane power until it was destroyed from its own power and lost to the sands of time."

"So, a four-thousand-year-old scroll even says it is lost."

"There are clues in the text. 'Sands' of time has to mean something," Amasis replied.

"That's just an expression," Lestrade said, but she stopped when she saw Amasis smiling. "You're still smiling. What's with that smile?"

"We have more," Amasis said.

"More outlandish theories."

Amasis held his grin. "An explorer returned."

"What?"

"He is in the infirmary, and he is babbling about demons and warlocks, but he returned with a tale and a general location," Amasis said.

Lestrade lowered her head. "An insane explorer, his mind burned from the sun, has said a general location? Where?" Lestrade asked.

Amasis grinned. "Nou Món, the *Island of the Throne.*"

* * * * *

(EONS in the Past)

In the days before the old gods fell to the mortal world, mortals lived in harmony with the natural world and the beast that roamed it. All mortal beings were one. Life was peaceful.

When the mortals we now call ancient would come to the end of their lives, they would venture to what was grasslands and there they fell and died. It was their time to pass on from one life and into the next, but for them that next life was within the earth.

In earthen tombs they laid for generations and offered their mortal vessels to the world so that a new generation could inherit it. From their remains sprang up a forest, ancient and mystical. Those trees were tall and strong, flowering with an abundance of vegetation. Those that walked through the forest felt its power and sought the wisdom of the trees, for within that forest magic spoke to the mortals. Great chiefs and shamans would walk through the forests, learning all they could. Men and elves would commune with one another. Quarmi and Orc came together under the banners of brotherhood.

Such was the way for the mortals of old. That was life during the Arcane Age.

For many millennia, that forest was celebrated and worshipped for its great magic, and it was that magic that attracted the fallen children of the Creator. It was that ancient and mystical forest that was destroyed by the great energy that was the old gods, those fallen children when they arrived on the mortal plain.

The mortals used the forest's timber, filled with powerful magic and wisdom, which now laid broken, to build the great city for these heavenly beings. The rocks and mud, filled with the blood and tears of the ancients, made the mortar between the city's bricks. Stones from the primordial mountains, the first home of mortals, rose to new heights with stone laid upon stone. It was a city like no other. In those days, great cities had grown, but this was not a city for mortals. The spires reached the heavens, while the temples dwarfed anything made prior. They cast statues in gold as tributes to the new divine overlords. In the center of this majestic metropolis stood a tower that reached higher than any other spire. Rising above the clouds as if the old gods wished to return to the heavens whence they fell.

A city of marble, silver, and gold built for gods and beings of supreme magic to rule over mortals for all time. A city built to corrupt mortal kind with luxury and wonder.

Slowly, the mortals turned from the Creator, who they once revered. Forgetting their past, the mortals fought and battled each other for the attention and affection of these new divine beings. They forgot the old ways that had kept them safe and peaceful. Soon, corruption spread across the lands. It was a plague that festered in the hearts and souls of every living being, even in the ground where the forest once stood.

The remnants of the forest that was destroyed so long ago wept in sorrow from beyond the spirit world. It could feel the hatred that permeated its lands. The fallen children, the gods of mortals, were tainting all that the forest had meant to the mortals, their kinfolk. The souls of those that had passed on to the spirit world had one last gasp of magic remaining. The roots were still strong and with the help of a mortal man, a human mage called Viri Al Sim, they sent away the fallen children to a plane beyond the mortal realm. It was then that the lands tore apart, falling into the ocean, creating the island of Nou Món.

It was there that Viri Al Sim watched the old gods fade from existence and there he remained to stand guard over the island for all time.

An island lost within the sands of time that no mortal could now find. Cut off from the rest of existence and only found through the greatest of means and sacrifices. A magical land that only magical blood could find. What riches lay untouched, no one could say. Though many had heard fables of great stores of wealth, technologies, and power. It was a fool's errand and a dead man's quest.

Viri Al Sim knew the prophecy foretold of one that would come and break the barrier between the mortal world and the realm of the old gods. If one was strong enough to break such a powerful magical barrier, then they could control the will of the old gods, and the mortal world would face its greatest threat.

IN THE MEANTIME

In the days since the Shrouded Guild defeated the mage Braga, and saved the world, their numbers grew, though gradually. Aklima took Uldin north to train as a ranger, and help the people defend themselves against the Huns. Sabutai, now married to Hitomi, traveled south to reestablish the Mage Guild after Obed's death. However, before leaving Lotcala to join Sabutai, Hitomi recruited a couple of new members into their guild. These members, including the new ones that Aklima and Uldin could bring in, helped to provide a base of operations for the guild. It also provided for some benefits to begin its work.

Hitomi and Sabutai changed the order's mode of operation to ensure safety, security and, most of all, secrecy. They added secret calls and responses to allow members who had never met to know that they could talk with one hundred percent honesty and trust.

The original members of the Shrouded Guild learned in the years since Braga's defeat just how complicated the world was. Ionius taunted Sabutai that the young mage did not know how the world worked. That much was true. Sabutai and his guild thought their job would be to protect the world against the machinations of evil mortals and old gods. Soon, they learned that there were many more powers at work. Thankfully, the Shrouded Guild would gain some allies in their tasks, but also enemies. Other clandestine orders had taken to the work of either protecting the world or seeing it destroyed.

Newer members also possessed many more skill sets, a key recruiting factor. Artisans, mages, thieves, and even assassins were sought after. People who knew the value of discretion were the obvious choices. This also allowed funds to fill the coffers. Bringing in members with expertise in economic dealings was a blessing for the young guild. However, the goal was to keep the membership numbers to a select few. Survival depended on it. So, Hitomi decided, with fellow member approval, that the best way to stay in business was to charge a fee for services rendered. Gold guaranteed loyalty.

Six years after the order was established, the membership had climbed to twenty-one and Hitomi, in her role as the guild-master, wanted to keep it at that number for the duration. Sabutai was busy in his role as Grand Mage of the Mage Order, more than happy to pass the guild-master position to his wife.

Word was soon getting back to Hitomi of disturbances in the south and east, in further off lands that the guild had yet touched. However, within her reach was a guild associate, a merchant that had been a valuable asset and alley but never officially joined. That merchant, Marcus, had provided intelligence that many beasts turning far more aggressive than their usual nature. Something was driving them towards the human settlements, and this was bad for Marcus' business, and of course, for the mortals living in the areas. While it wasn't a hardline rule that these beasts were children of the old gods, more than a few were. That is why Hitomi saw the guild's intervention as necessary.

Hitomi strolled passed mages as she walked the Mage Guild's hallways. Some mages gave her friendly nods of recognition and others shot inquisitive looks, both of which she ignored. They were marveling at her grey skin and ornate mouth and nose covering. None of that bothered her or even registered in her mind. Her only concern was her destination, and that was the office at the end of the hall. It was the office of her husband, Sabutai.

A comfortable room, red brick walls with a white plaster covering the old bricks, vaulted ceiling for air circulation in the warm climate. The room was full of colored mosaics and other designs of kaleidoscopic patterns adorning the space. Hitomi opened the door and stepped onto the sewn rugs as she made her way to her husband's desk. He was on the balcony overlooking the city.

"You're here because of the manticore attacks," he said. He didn't have to ask; he could almost read his wife's mind. "You wish to send the guild in?"

"Have you been practicing your telepathy or are you wearing a fluorite gem?" Hitomi quipped, taking a seat in front of Sabutai's desk.

Sabutai walked in from the balcony and sat in the chair next to his wife, reaching for her hand. "Fluorite is for protecting against vampires and mind readers," Sabutai heaved a sigh. "You are the leader of the guild. You don't have to come to me for anything, you know."

His greying hair fell to his eyes, and he pulled it to the side. In the time since he had become the Grand Mage, he had aged. The stress of his dual roles was taking its toll.

Hitomi smiled at her husband. "I don't, but you're my husband, and I love you," she saw Sabutai's smile. "Also, I trust your opinion and your insight on such matters. Have you been able to see anything through the Thin Place?"

Sabutai's smile faded, and the mage grew grim. "Nothing good. There is something dark behind a veil that I can't see beyond."

"Then I guess it'll take people on the ground to figure it out," Hitomi responded.

"So, what is your plan?"

"I'm sending two of our guild members to investigate the attacks and see what's behind it. Marcus can ferry them and provide some added insights." Hitomi replied.

Sabutai nodded. "You're thinking of sending the assassin?"

"She's reliable and gets the job done with incredible efficiency. She and another agent should be enough. I'd like to send a mage, if possible," Hitomi smiled. "It's just a fact-finding mission, anyway. Her skills will be useful in staying hidden and getting out quickly. The mage can provide valuable help, just in case things go south. I'm thinking Nash."

Sabutai let go of his wife's hand and got up from his seat. Walking to his desk, he retrieved a scroll. "Where is your closest healer, or any registered mage? Nash is skilled, but he left the guild before finishing his studies, and healing wasn't his strongest suit, if I recall."

Hitomi thought for a moment. "We have a mage in Anavai. A healer named Ko. It'll take him time to get to Castemont, but that's the best idea I have at the moment, but you already know that."

Sabutai looked at Hitomi, but he still didn't smile. "I do. I also have a request." He walked up to Hitomi and handed her a scroll. "This is a mage we have here at the guild. Baron Donal Hardstone of Lotcala sent her here to train.

Her name is Cailin Fare, and she might prove useful."

"There's something else. Has to be. Hardstone has guilds that can train young mages, so why is she different?" Hitomi read Sabutai's face well enough to know he was withholding information.

Sabutai sighed. "We noted she has peculiar traits. One such trait that might be useful for this mission is that she speaks to animals."

"With rune stones?" Hitomi asked.

With the power of rune stones, though rare, a user could learn the spells used to speak to the beasts of the world for a short amount of time.

"No," Sabutai replied with a furrowed brow.

"That's a dark mark," Hitomi said, opening the scroll. Her eyes showed her shock. "Sabutai, these are dangerous abilities."

"Plants wilt and die when she is around for lengthy periods of time. She doesn't sacrifice them or anything, they just die," Sabutai said, elaborating on what was written on the scroll Hitomi was reading. "We believe we've been able to get her to control that, but it's a natural ability. She is also quite capable of dream glimpsing and bewilderment. Again, naturally. There have been... incidents, though very accidental on her part. It's been some time since we've had any incident."

"Sabutai…" Hitomi began. "Those are dark marks. Anytime a mage can enter a dream and make the dreamer do something, then that's considered dark! Accident or not, they will figure out how that works, and it's not long before an accident becomes an intentional act," Hitomi rose and tried to hand the scroll back to Sabutai, but the mage refused it.

"She can be of use with the beasts."

"She could also kill my agents!" Hitomi yelled.

Sabutai clasped his wife's arms, trying to comfort her. "I wouldn't ask this if I thought that could happen. I will not see another mage fall to dark forces, but I think she is ready for a test. It's a quick mission, right?"

"That's the plan," Hitomi said stoically.

Sabutai tried to smile. "I'm not asking her to be a member, just given a chance to prove she can be out in the world. Each of those abilities, though dark, has opposite effects if we give the mage the ability to train in the proper use of magic."

Hitomi sat back down and Sabutai again sat next to her. "Have you ever seen anyone like this?" Hitomi asked.

Sabutai looked out towards the balcony. Hitomi could see his eyes water. "There was one," Sabutai began. "When I was a young mage, maybe only ten or eleven, another mage was taken from us. He was too powerful for the guild's teachers, and his power could not be contained. Obed took him away, but to be honest, I don't know what happened to him. He was a danger to everyone around him and he was in danger from outside forces, but no one tried to help him."

"So, you have tried to help her?" Hitomi asked.

"I have been able to help some, others have as well. It takes a village," Sabutai cracked a smile.

"Can she travel safely?"

Sabutai's smile grew. "She can. She's in her last year of training, and I think she'll be able to contain her powers effectively."

"Then send her to Castemont. She can meet with the other two agents there. Just tell her what to say," Hitomi sighed. She looked at Sabutai sternly. "She had better be ready."

Sabutai nodded. He hoped that she was.

THE SAME STORY, AN OLD STORY

Hammer strikes rang out from the shop of a simple orc blacksmith. Weaponsmith was his true training, but he would work many metals into all sorts of objects, so the term blacksmith was apt. Muscles tightened with each swing and the greenish hued skin glistened with sweat. Even when he dropped his hood to allow himself to cool, sweat still poured from his shaved head.

Behind him stood the bust of Dyos, the orc god of metalworkers. While many cultures in the world prayed to the old gods or to the Creator, orcs kept their own pantheon. Tsungo was no different in that regard. He, as he was a blacksmith, made sure to give thanks to Dyos each day for his skill and the many customers that crossed his threshold.

One such customer was the beautiful and altogether deadly rogue Ava. She always got her blades sharpened by the crafty orc, and that was nearly a weekly occurrence.

"Oi, Tsungo! I brought my blades for a quick honing before I sail out to Castemont," the raven-haired rogue handed her sheathed blades to the orc.

The knives were made with beautiful craftsmanship, curved for effective slashes but with enough of a point for deadly thrusts. Each blade, a twin set made of Wootz steel, were fourteen inches in length and each had an ebony hilt and jeweled pommels.

Tsungo took the blades in each hand and unsheathed them, one at a time, inspecting their wear. "Hmm," he murmured. "Fifty marks," the orc said, looking to Ava.

The rogue scrunched her nose at the amount. "Fifty marks?" she exclaimed. "I could take it to Fero and get them sharpened for barely a pence over thirty marks!"

Tsungo shoved the knives back toward Ava. "Then take them to Fero, and when his craftsmanship fails, you don't bother stepping back into my shop!"

Ava eyed the orc holding her knives. "Forty."

"Forty-five or leave," Tsungo replied coolly, pointing to the door.

"Fine forty-five marks, but they had better cut a bastard with just a glance."

Tsungo grinned. "You know my work well enough to know they will."

Ava smiled and then sat down on a nearby barrel as Tsungo went to work on her blades. "Thank you," she said, while inspecting her nails and digging soot from under her thumb.

"Yeah," Tsungo said quietly.

He was deep in thought and wasn't much for conversations anyway, but Ava was a bit more talkative.

"I've been coming here for nearly ten years and in those ten years, you've never asked me why I always need my blades sharpened. It's not that sharpening a blade is odd, just the frequency," Ava remarked.

"You're paying top silver for a service. The least I can do is keep my teeth together," Tsungo asked. "The coins change often, and that's peculiar, but the silver or gold has always weighed right, so I don't bother with the faces on the coins."

Ava grinned. "I got some ravens on me today. Good for some sport at the parlor down the street. You know the one? They serve the spiced rum from Kanakan and have plenty of pretty faces to spend time with."

"And to spend your coin on. I avoid spending money when I don't have to," Tsungo replied.

Ava put her hands behind her head and leaned back against the wall while sitting on the barrel. "Smart."

Ava had always admired the work of the orcs in the Freeholds, but Tsungo was different. Most orcs, hard workers and intelligent, were gifted craft workers, but Tsungo made metal objects that looked to be crafted by the gods. Tsungo's work was highly sought after, and he was always busy, but he made time for those he pegged as his friends.

The assassin patted her thighs and then stood up. "I'm going for a pint. See you in an hour or so?"

"Fine," Tsungo replied, glancing up as Ava walked out of his shop.

Ava walked down the street and at the first alleyway, she ducked in and pulled a small obsidian mirror from her pouch. "Ezhar Hitomi."

The mirror glowed for a few seconds before the Quarmi warrior appeared. "Ava. You have news?"

"Just prepping my blades for the trip and I'll be off on the last ship out of the port. However, I have an idea for a new contact."

"You know the idea behind recruiting," Hitomi replied.

"Yeah, I do, and I know an excellent craftsman when I see one. You said yourself that we need a reliable smithy," Ava smiled. "Well, I found one."

"Fine. Keep him in mind until you and Nash return from the mission. Then, and only then, will we see if he is worthy of joining us," Hitomi replied. "Good work Ava."

The mirror went black, and Ava smiled. "On to the bar."

* * * * *

Nash was a blonde headed mage that had been a mercenary swordsman in the years prior to joining the Shrouded Guild. While he had been a decent mage, his skill with a sword was what gave him his opportunities. It had been roughly seven or eight years. He couldn't remember how long since he had even checked into a guild-house and updated his credentials. Therefore, most people didn't even consider him as a mage. He was unregistered.

While the Knights of the Siler Seal experienced a major setback in Lotcala and other northern regions six years earlier, in Kargildan, the Knights still held onto their power. Nash was careful to conceal his arcane abilities, but his fame as a swordsman was the proverbial double-edged sword. Some who knew him as a swordsman also knew he was a mage. If too many connected the two identities, then he would be a target for the "holy" order. However, Nash was not someone that intelligent people would approach lightly. Too many would-be bandits made that mistake, but they didn't live for long afterward.

Nash's blue cloak concealed his baldric and sword, his hood pulled up over his head, while waiting on the dock. Others passed him by, not paying attention to the man, ordinary looking as he was. He was getting ready to board a ship, destined for Castemont, but first he had to wait for someone.

The woman Nash had been waiting on appeared a few moments after the last passenger, besides Nash, boarded the ship.

"Hawks fly east on cold days," she whispered.

"And falcons fly west on warm nights," Nash replied. "You took your time," Nash quipped.

The woman, dressed in black, smiled. "I like to be unseen when speaking with guild members," she smiled, a smile that left Nash uneasy.

She was as deadly as anyone he knew, more so than Ava even. He could feel her powers and her skill. She was a Blackbird, a woman trained in deadly martial arts and necromancy. She wore the color of her trade, a long black tunic down to her knees with tight-fitting pants. Her leather sandals were endued with magic to be silent with each step. On her head was a black veil. She marked her hands and forearms with tattoos. Most people thought of them as pretty images or designs, but Nash recognized their true nature, necromancy and other spells. Magic was her craft, unregistered, of course.

"What do I need to know?" Nash asked.

"Something is brewing in the south and east. Someone seeks to uproot established teachings and they are using others for their own devices. The manticore attacks and the griffin slayings are part of a larger plan by a dark force."

Nash smirked. "That must make you happy."

The Blackbird's smile faded. "I do not wish for chaos for the sake of chaos. Blackbirds cause chaos for a purpose. The world only works when things change. Change is chaos and chaos is our religion," she turned to see something that caught her sight from the corner of her eye.

Satisfied that nothing was there, the woman turned back to Nash.

"Someone is controlling the beasts for their own gain, but not for the glory of anything I serve."

"I just assumed..." Nash began.

"My powers are dark, but not unnatural. People *assume* we are evil, but believe me when I say there is no good or evil in the world, only cause and effect.

Raging beasts help nothing," the Blackbird replied with a sneer.

"Sorry," Nash replied. He pulled out a silver coin. "Thank you for your service."

"Keep your coin. There is something else," the woman said, putting her hand on top of Nash's.

The man could see the intricate and ornate tattooed spells, and it gave him a shiver.

"Okay. What else is there?" Nash asked.

"Your master is sending a young mage to meet you and Ava in Castemont," the Blackbird smiled, pulling her hand away and back to the folds of her tunic. "A mage that is a mystery even to my sisters and their eyes. Your master named her Cailin Fare from Hardstone."

She never called Hitomi anything other than 'your master'. She wanted to accentuate the fact that she was not a true member of the guild and only an associate.

"Why is that such a big deal?" Nash smirked.

The Blackbird grinned menacingly. "My sisters didn't know much about her, but I do. She's a dark marked mage. She can glimpse dreams and drain life."

That was a dangerous combination, and Nash wasn't happy to have had that information kept from his last briefing with

Hitomi. Nash looked at the Blackbird and frowned at the woman's delight.

"That makes you happy?" Nash asked.

"I gave my life over to black magic from birth, so to find another mage so naturally talented in the art is a blessing for my kind. Though she is naïve and easily swayed on another path. Be careful, Nash, your master fears this mage," the Blackbird replied. "Perhaps you should as well."

Behind Nash, the captain of the ship called out to him to board. Nash turned and waved to the captain that he acknowledged the order. "Thanks for the warning," Nash began as he turned back to the Blackbird. "What else..."

The woman was gone.

"I hate it when she does that," Nash remarked before boarding the ship.

* * * * *

"Are all of our plans in place?" An elf lord asked his companion.

"Yes, my lord. The forge is prepared and once Geddoe brings us the dragon he captured, we will forge a new weapon." The second elf replied.

"Why trust such an uncouth human like Geddoe?" the elf lord asked with a turned-up nose.

The companion smiled. "My lord Marscal, the work for this new weapon is the goal. A goal which requires a dragon and Geddoe is the finest dragon hunter and trapper. His work is solely for our gain."

Marscal, an elder high elf with greying hair, eyed his younger companion. "If that dragon isn't up to the task or doesn't live long enough, Persa, you will pay for it."

Persa, the younger elf companion, grimaced at the words. "Understood, my lord."

"Good. Now my master can do what Braga was too weak to accomplish," Marscal grinned.

The two elves walked out to the busy market street, leaving the large estate behind. Marscal was a high elf, the most populous of the elven races. Persa was a sand elf, and they were usually despised, but in the eastern kingdoms sand elves were more welcomed. Persa stepped into the light of the midday sun. Her tan skin glistened as the sun shone on her.

Persa wrapped a cloth around her head. "My lord, take care for the sun here in Tyranos bites much harder than in the north and west were your kind hails from."

Tyranos was a bustling trading center, but it was in the heart of the Shifting Sands, a desert that bordered the Jagged Mountains and was known for its high temperatures. Mostly, the area was inhospitable, but Tyranos had a cool flowing river that fed into its oasis. This made life a bit more bearable. The people that lived in the area wore looser fitting, light fabrics to combat the heat and most covered their heads from the sun.

Marscal sneered. "The day I take the advice of a sand elf is the day I will bow down to a dwarf!" The proud elf walked out into the open and let the sun hit him. He felt the sting of the light and the heat of the desert, but he ignored both. "This is where my master will make his kingdom. It would benefit me to get used to this climate," he said finally.

Persa grinned. "Indeed, my lord, indeed."

"Now, find me a smith worthy of forging such a magnificent weapon," Marscal said, looking back to Persa.

"I know just the orc," the sand elf grinned wickedly.

* * * * *

Cailin Fare was packing her satchel when Sabutai and Hitomi visited her chambers. Cailin wasn't sure why she'd been moved into a private room several years prior, but she was grateful. Her guild-mates were grateful as well. In reality, it was a policy for those marked as being dark mages, though it was a new policy. In the time before Sabutai took over the guild, they expelled dark mages. History repeatedly showed that was a mistake.

"Cailin?" Sabutai smiled as he knocked on the wooden door.

The young mage answer with a beaming smile. "Grand Mage! What a surprise! Here to see me off?" the young mage let Sabutai and his wife in.

"It's something like that," Sabutai tried his best to smile, but it was difficult because of the weight of the task. "Hitomi has a few words for you before you go." Sabutai looked at his wife.

With the Quarmi's normally stern demeanor, she eyed the mage. "I want to make sure we prepared you before leaving."

Cailin smiled. "Oh, yes ma'am. I have just finished packing and the Grand Mage told me the exact words to say. Grasses on the pla—"

"Shhh!" Hitomi hissed, putting her hand up, silencing Cailin, who stood there in shock. "I'm certain he prepped you well enough on what to say, however," she stopped and looked around with a bit of confusion. "Why do you have four large bags?"

Cailin snapped out of her trance. "Oh! This is just in case. You never know when you might need the stuff you never think about. I have gowns for formal occasions, hot, and cool nights. I also packed some books in case I need to do some research," Cailin looked to Hitomi, more than perplexed. "Is this too much?"

Hitomi glared at Cailin. "You will take one bag and only one bag. You will travel as light as possible. This is in and out!"

"But ma'am..."

Hitomi stopped the young mage again, put her hands on Cailin's shoulders and gripped her tightly. "The people you are meeting in Castemont are killers, trained and remorseless. They will protect you as a favor to me, but if you slow them to the point of putting their lives in danger, they will not think twice about leaving you. Cailin, I must know that if you go, that you are willing to do the same."

Cailin looked confused and scared. "I... I thought this was a research expedition. Grand Mage?" she said, looking to Sabutai.

Sabutai lowered his head and sighed. "Cailin, you can understand animals of all sorts, and that is a skill that will probably be essential to the success of this mission. However, this is something that can easily turn into a life threating journey. Hitomi and I must know that you are prepared."

Cailin lowered her head and sniffed, drawing back a sob. She tried to hide her emotions. "You're sending me because I'm dark marked," she did not have to ask. She knew the answer well enough.

Cailin heard the whispers daily as she passed people in the halls, and she knew why no one wanted to spend time with her anymore. She tossed her satchel onto her bed and dropped on the mattress. "This is what I'm good for, I guess. Speaking to animals and killing plants," she looked over to a few pots on the windowsill holding wilted plants and sniffed again.

Sabutai shook his head, but Hitomi rushed in before he could speak.

"You are unique in your skillsets. You have abilities that scare others and skills that worry me, but these are skills that few others have. There are things you can do that might save lives. Hitomi said. "Dark mages don't normally choose that option. In fact, I know of only one other, Balt."

"Balt the Blessed? He was a dark mage?" Cailin asked. She was from the Kingdom of Lotcala, and every Lotcalan knew Balt's story. "How could he have been a dark mage? The Creator blessed him," Cailin glanced up to Sabutai.

"Hell if I know. I'm from here, I don't really know Balt." Sabutai said.

Hitomi shot her husband an irritated stare. "Balt was an explorer and a mage from Lotcala. He professed the old gods, and it wasn't until after his death did the people tie him to the Creator. The truth was something worse."

Hitomi sat next to Cailin. "If memory serves me, he was run0 off from his home because he was a dark mage and because of his belief in the old gods. That was still common for the Gota in those days. He killed someone and was sentenced to death, but he escaped and was branded a pariah. However, he spent his life doing great works for people with the gifts, though dark, which he was born with. He turned himself from a criminal into a hero. That's why he is called blessed. At least, that's the legend that everyone always says."

"You can save lives on this mission and be a hero like Balt, but it's up to you to choose. Life is going to give you many choices and most will be easy, but once in a while you will be handed a difficult choice. A choice that is the difference between life and death, sometimes your life and someone else's death. You must be able to choose." Hitomi finished.

Hitomi stood. "Do you understand?"

Cailin looked at Hitomi and then at Sabutai. "I understand," she said, standing up. She reached over, picked up her satchel, and then threw a few other garments inside. "I'll take this bag and be on my way."

Hitomi nodded as did Sabutai, but the Grand Mage's face showed his fear. "Tread carefully Cailin. You have a great power within you, and we have trained you as well as the guild can train you. Just remember that once you leave the guild, the path you take is completely up to you."

"Yes, Grand Mage," Cailin replied before the three left the room. Just a second later, Cailin rushed back into her room and retrieved a large book, Lady Emilia Chisui's *Field Guide to Beasts*, before rushing back out.

ESCAPE

Waves lapped the sides of an oak hulled ship. Clear skies accompanied by a strong eastwardly breeze propelled the trade ship onward. Marcus walked the length of his galley, a fine ship with a hundred oars, not the biggest galley on the waters, but certainly not the smallest. Marcus was proud of his ship. It was faster than most and it could carry more goods than other galleries, which wasn't saying much, but the ship's speed meant he could gain more wealth by sailing on more voyages. That was his principal goal in life.

Marcus grew up in the slums of Devos and saw a better future for himself and his family on the seas. Life and fate, however, had other plans. While Marcus saw the sea as a source of riches, his brother squandered what little Marcus could send home and soon debts to very shady and dangerous people mounted. Marcus returned home to find his family murdered and his money gone. He also learned of a price on his head for his brother's unpaid debts. That did not sit well with the grief-stricken man. Still, he was in no position to do anything else but run and run he did. Since that fateful day, Marcus had not set foot in Devos.

Instead, he used his skills to become a successful merchant captain. Away from Devos, Marcus was protected by his many contacts and customers. Even underworld crime kingpins like Bakare, the ruler of Devos' vast criminal empire, could not touch him now.

The expert captain, on the seas now for over twenty years, smiled looking down the length of the ship. "A good wind is all I need to make my life complete."

At his side walked the statuesque Venera. Marcus' most trusted companion and first mate was another reason why crime lords like Bakare stayed away.

Venera was a deadly Stone Elf that Marcus had saved from execution by simply purchasing her from the slave market in Rapanoq, a large port city west of the Southern Kingdoms. Marcus, however, was not in the habit of keeping slaves, so he freed the woman, his intention the entire time. Venera had other plans. She stuck close to Marcus and soon became a valued partner and a skilled sailor.

"The winds have been favorable, captain," Venera replied to her captain. "We should reach Castemont by midday tomorrow."

Marcus sniffed the air and laughed. "I can already smell the oiled iron of the knights' armor."

Marcus wasn't fond of the Knights of the Silver Seal, but he was fond of their gold and silver, made from his shipments to the knights. Mostly iron ore and letters from their homes. He also enjoyed having the knights as back up since they were fond of him. Mostly.

Venera went back to her tasks as Marcus watched the sea move all around him. He had promised his crew shore leave in Castemont. However, he and Venera would be busy, a favor to Hitomi. They would lead her agents into Kargildan. Marcus walked back to the stern where the captain's berth was located. The captain sat and poured a cup of port wine. Venera rejoined him a short while later.

"Captain," the Stone Elf began, taking a seat next to him. "Is it safe for us both to leave the crew alone in Castemont? It is a major port for the Knights of the Silver Seal. They might get rowdy being away from land so long."

"Exactly. What better place to leave them?" Marcus smiled. "Hitomi wanted me to sail into Blizzard Bay and dock in Ur Gildan. I disagreed with the Quarmi lord and told her that, given the time of year and the populace, that Castemont was the best port of call. After some thought, she agreed, but it does mean more walking than I prefer. Still, Castemont is much more secure, and I think the crew would do better with knightly supervision."

Marcus, always a couple of steps ahead, was banking on the knightly order's unwitting help, and it had worked in the past. He knew he had to meet with three of Hitomi's agents, well, two agents and another associate, and he knew he had to get them to Reposo. There were plenty of ways to get to the small northern town, but those methods decreased in number depending on the season. The Bay of Blizzards was aptly named. For five months of the year, the bay was nearly unnavigable because of the sea ice and heavy storms. That time was fast approaching and Marcus' galley, a brave and true ship she was, wasn't fit for such a voyage.

Marcus picked up a lute and strummed a few cords. Venera closed her eyes and let the tune take her away, to a past that she had left behind the day they stole away her from her family. A tear rolled down her cheek.

Marcus stopped his playing. "I'm sorry," he said, lowering the instrument.

"It's quite alright," Venera replied, opening her eyes. "It's reminding me of a lullaby that I used to sing to my children years ago."

Marcus was the only one that knew the tale of Venera's past and her family. In the years since they had sailed together, they had visited many slave markets in search of her family members, but they never found anyone other than a few other Elves that had lived in the same village. Never anything more than rumors.

Marcus put a comforting hand on to Venera's hand. "We'll find them," he smiled.

Venera returned the smile. "I know, captain," she rose from the seat. "I'll make my rounds now and join you for our meal," Marcus nodded in reply as the Elf walked off.

* * * * *

Nash was already in Castemont for nearly three full days before Ava poked her head around a corner and picked him of his coin pouch. A game she liked to play with other agents to let them know she was more than a pretty face.

"You know that isn't funny," Nash sneered.

"To you it isn't. I find it rather hilarious," Ava grinned and laughed.

Nash snatched his coin pouch out of Ava's open palm and walked on.

"Things are a bit more serious than you seem to think, Ava," Nash grabbed Ava's arm and pulled her around the corner of a nearby building.

Ava looked at the man in anger, but Nash let go and began to explain.

"I'm sure Hitomi told you just as much as she told me about this third wheel we're taking along. "Something about her being a mage and a favor to Sabutai. I don't get paid to ask too many questions, Nash. Neither do you," Ava replied, sounding annoyed.

"A little birdie gave me more insight on our new companion."

Ava scoffed. "You trust that woman?" Ava had a long-standing hatred for the Blackbirds and what they stood for. "They will tell you whatever sounds good to get your allegiance and then cut your throat once you've given them what they want. I've seen it happen to stronger willed men than you."

"I'll pretend that a hired assassin's opinion of me isn't insulting, and just say that this Blackbird is one that I trust. More than other people I know, especially," Nash retorted.

"Fine, then what did she say?"

"This mage, Cailin Fare, is dark marked," Nash responded in a whisper.

Ava stood there inquisitively. She wanted to know more, but she was certain that Nash wouldn't know anymore and that if Hitomi had told him differently than her, then he would have gloated over her.

"So, then what do we do when we meet up with her? Also, isn't that any minute? The ship from Kalisadad was docking when you caught up to me a short while ago."

"We can't let her know that we know at first, but we will need to watch her closely," Nash replied. "I don't enjoy being left in the dark like this, and I'd rather her confess it."

Ava nodded. "Why would Hitomi send a dark marked mage?"

"As you said, Hitomi is doing a favor for Sabutai," Nash shook his head. "Never do business with spouses. See, this is why I never got married."

"Sure. This is why," Ava rolled her eyes. "Let's head to the pier that the ship was coming to and find her. Hitomi vouched for her and that has always been good enough for me and should be for you, too."

Nash nodded, and the two went back to the docks to find Cailin.

It was the busy season for spice and ore offloading in the southern regions. Not only that, the sea air was mixing with the strange foreign aromas. Most were used to it, but for the new visitors, it might have been off-putting. Nash and Ava were used to docks. They had no problem walking around the fishmongers, and others who smelled of the briny sea. The pier for Cailin's ship was rather busy that day, but the pair managed to get there just as an obvious mage, and an inexperienced spy, was making her way, asking everyone she bumped into if they were Nash and or Ava.

Ava dropped her head. "Kids."

"She's at least twenty from what Hitomi said. This sort of behavior is from too many years of training in the guild. She should know not to talk to strangers," Nash replied in a monotone voice. "Come on, let's introduce ourselves."

The two walked to the obviously lost woman and stopped her. "Miss, I believe we are the ones you're looking for."

Cailin looked at Nash and Ava, squinted and then shook her head. "No, because you didn't say the words. The Grand Mage said that you would say."

"The dew falls only on moonless nights," Nash interrupted.

"Uhhh. No." Cailin replied, raising an eyebrow.

"You forgot the greeting?" Ava asked with a chuckle.

Nash turned to Ava and threw his hands in the air. "There are so many, and Hitomi keeps changing them. How can I remember them all?" he cried.

Ava waved the man off and then looked at Cailin. "The moon is new this night."

Cailin smiled. "Grasses on the plains will receive little dew," the young mage's smile grew. "Hi! I'm Cailin!" she exclaimed.

"I'm Ava, and this genius here is Nash," the assassin replied, pointing to herself and her partner. "We have a hotel room not far, and tomorrow Marcus will join us."

Cailin, still smiling, followed the pair to the hotel. Nash, still annoyed, keeps an eye glancing behind him just in case.

At the inn, the three sat by a roaring hearth drinking ale and wine in the tavern hall on the first floor of the inn. A server came by and placed a plate of olives, bread, and cheeses down in between them. She also brought over a tankard of wine for the table. "Ale will be brought over soon. Just filling the tankards," the server said before walking off.

Cailin took the tankard and refilled her cup. Ava eyed the younger woman carefully. She wasn't as suspicious as Nash. Ava had the confidence to do what was necessary, if need be, to save her life. Nash's too, if it was a benefit in any way to her.

"Cailin?" Ava spoke up. "I'd be lying if I said I wasn't surprised that they sent you here to us."

Cailin looked up at Ava and nodded. "I was a bit surprised to be sent out like this as well. Most mages get assigned to other mage guilds or in towns, not as envoys like this. I thought I'd be sent to some hospital as a healer or to work in a funerary hall."

"Then why were you sent to us?" Ava asked, narrowing her eyes. "In your opinion, that is."

Cailin lowered her eyes. "The Grand Mage and Hitomi thought it would be wise to bring a mage along," she said softly.

Nash scoffed before taking a gulp of his ale. The server returned with ale, taking the empty wine tankard from the table. Nash followed the server's movements, admiring her ample form.

He looked at his two companions. "If you both will excuse me. I think I might be in more exciting company elsewhere," he then stood and walked over to the woman and began his best efforts to flirt with her.

Ava rolled her eyes. "Ass," she chuckled, and then turned back to Cailin. "You're not just a mage, are you?"

"I'm not sure what you mean."

Ava shook her head. "You were sent because you're a dark mage, aren't you?"

"They told you?" Cailin said, her eyes watering.

"No, and your first lesson is to make sure you have ways of getting the information that your superiors don't want to tell you. The second lesson needs to be how to keep that information to yourself. You should have denied it," Ava replied, leaning back in her chair and drinking her wine. Ava pointed to Nash at the bar nearby. "Nash has some shadier contacts than what Hitomi would like, but the lady comes through with valuable information, and she knew you were dark marked."

"I've never done any of the dark magic on purpose," Cailin said in a hushed voice.

"Is that supposed to make me feel safer?" Ava asked, smirking at the younger woman.

"I'm not sure. I just wanted you to know that I'm not a danger to you or Nash."

Ava leaned over the table and with her finger motioned Cailin closer. "Time will tell if you are a danger to us. If you are, I'll slit your throat and leave you where you fall. Did Hitomi or Sabutai tell you what I do for a living?"

The obviously scared mage just shook her head softly.

Ava gave a quick and curt nod. "Suffice it to say that I have plenty of experience in that sort of thing. I can be your friend, or I can be your enemy. It's all up to your future decisions."

Nash suddenly returned to the table. "We have to go! Marcus moored his ship and docked early, but there's some problems with the Silver Seal boys."

The three rushed up to their room to gather their belongings. A good thing they all packed light. However, the brief time they had to run to the room was all it took for several knights to barge into the inn demanding the owner to hand over the mage. They stood in the hallway, listening to the rush of more knights barging into the inn.

"How did they find out she was a mage?" Ava whispered. She looked at Cailin, but the young mage just shrugged.

Nash peered around the corner of the hallway wall just outside of their room. "They must have seen the passenger manifest of her ship and then leaned on the captain. Odds are Sabutai purchased the fare and that would point to a mage on the ship somewhere. Even if it was Hitomi, with all that happened six years ago, they would be hunting anyone connected to her as well," Nash looked around. "We'll have to go out the window," he said, motioning for his companions to head back.

The three rushed back to their room. Ava poked her head out of the window. They were on the side of the building with a dark alley below them.

"We can shimmy down the balcony post and run over to the docks. If we're quick, we'll make it out, but what do we do when we get to Marcus?" Ava said.

Nash began to climb out of the window. "We'll figure that out once we get to him," the nimble man began his descent down the wooden post, holding the balcony up.

Once on the ground, Nash scouted the area and motioned for his companions once the coast was clear.

"You go down first," Ava said to Cailin.

The younger woman shook her head.

"Look," Ava snapped. "If you're caught up here alone, then they will kill you. If they find me, I'm not a mage and I can take care of myself anyway. Now go."

Cailin made her way to the post and crawled over the railing, gripping the wood tightly. She inched down the post, the heels of her leather boots digging into the post with each movement.

"Dammit girl! We don't have time for you to be scared!" Nash quietly exclaimed up to Cailin.

The scared mage inched further down but was still at too slow of a pace for Nash.

"Dammit!" he said.

Ava hopped over the railing and shimmied down the opposite post. "Just like this, Cailin," she said before landing on her feet. "Come on, or we're gone!"

Cailin eased her grip on the post and let herself fall. Thankfully, for her sake, Nash was below her. The older man caught Cailin and then eased her on to the stone street.

"Fine. Now that's done, let's get over to the Marcus' ship," Nash said.

"No," Ava replied, stopping the man. "They'll be watching the docks. We must get out of town."

"What about Marcus?" Cailin asked.

"He's not a mage, and I doubt he is travelling with one. He'll be fine and we'll figure out a way to meet up with him later," Ava answered.

"A way out?" Nash questioned. "I might know a way if it is still a secret. An old smuggler's tunnel from before the knights took the city over. If it is still undiscovered, then we can get out and walk towards the north."

* * * * *

At that moment on the docks, Marcus was watching groups of knights and their men at arms running back and forth around the town. Several had already stopped by his ship, and they cleared it more times than he cared to count. Retainers for the Knights of the Silver Seal stood guarding the docks, checking on anyone coming toward the ships. Marcus knew his companions could not board until the commotion and the guards were gone.

"Someone said something," Marcus said to Venera, standing next to him. "We must reach them another way."

"The guards will let no one off the ships, nor will they let people leave the town," Venera replied.

"True, and if we try to sail out of port, they'll pull the port's chains and rip my ship to shreds. We're stuck here for the duration of whatever this is?" Marcus said with an obvious dejected tone to his voice.

Marcus and his ship were stuck, but not without options. He walked to his cabin and picked up a few important items, stashing them into a rucksack. Before walking out of his cabin, he grabbed a sack of gold.

"Come Venera. We've a mission to complete and there's trouble to be found."

"The knights?" Venera asked as the two walked down the gangplank towards the dock.

"That's what this little bag is for," Marcus grinned and strolled up to the two men guarding the dock he was moored at.

After a quick conversation, the captain smiled, handed the gold over and motioned for Venera to join him. The two guards stepped aside for her. Marcus and Venera walked through the town, watching out for their passengers, but all they saw was the commotion of the knights running through the area, dragging people out of taverns and inns.

"Damn hypocrites," Venera scoffed, watching the knights pulling a prostitute from a brothel. "I'd bet good coin that they visited her not even a fortnight ago."

"True, but these aren't the same sort of knights you'd find in the mainland cities. These are the men that are conscripted or sold into the order," Marcus answered back. "Here these men are the criminals or poorer subjects of other nations and kingdoms," he looked around. "Nash and Ava are too smart to stick around in this.

Knowing Nash, he will have taken the smugglers' tunnels."

The pair walked away from the growing riot and went to the older section of town, where the tunnels were hidden.

Marcus knew the way to the tunnels. He had used them twice throughout his career. The path was always the same, and the tunnels were hidden in plain sight. However, as he and Venera approached, he noticed something was amiss.

"Someone has recently moved these boards," Marcus said. He looked around the area, but everything was quiet. "Someone is in the tunnels."

"Could it be Nash and Ava?" Venera asked.

Marcus pursed his lips. "Let's hope so. This is the first way I'd think of getting out of town and I know Nash knows this way," Marcus grinned at Venera. "I showed it to him a few years ago," Marcus pulled his seax knife from his belt. "Just in case."

Venera followed close behind, also with a blade drawn, just in case. The only light the pair had was scant moonlight or a street torch lamp piercing through the street drains.

Further down the tunnel they could hear what they thought were whispers. Whether or not they were indeed whispers, the two kept their own pace. If the knights had in fact discovered the tunnels, then of those whispers were their voices. That meant that Marcus and Venera would probably have to fight their way out of the tunnels.

The tunnels narrowed ahead and soon a fork was coming. Marcus knew the way. The two were crouched, moving slowly and down the left fork. The whispers grew louder. Bits of conversation could be heard from further up the tunnel. The people that were in front of them had to of known of the correct path at the fork. Marcus breathed a little easier. That was a pretty confident sign of a smuggler or Nash.

He kept walking, leading Venera deeper until they came to the end of the tunnel. A ladder led them up to a small shack just on the outskirts of the town.

Marcus climbed out, looked around, and saw it was empty. He helped Venera out, and the two walked outside and into the cool night air.

"They must have come this way," Venera said. Marcus nodded to her. "We can try to catch their trail. I'm sure they will stop to rest," He finished.

Marcus looked around. He wasn't a tracker, but Venera could do better on dry land. She found the trail in a less than a minute. They ran off in the same direction as the footprints. Three sets heading north. Thirty minutes later, the pair reached a small grove of trees where a campfire had been lit. It was far enough away from the city that the danger was minimal. Marcus walked through the brush, rousing Ava and Cailin. Nash stepped up from around a tree and put a blade to the captain's neck. Venera put hers to Nash's.

"And here I thought we were friends," Marcus quipped to Venera.

Ava jumped up. "Marcus!"

Nash pulled back his blade. "Sorry, but it's hard to see in the firelight against the new moon. Come on and sit with us." He looked at Venera and smiled as she sheathed her blade that she had held at his stomach.

Everyone sat around the fire and rested in the peaceful forest. It was not the night they had in mind, but at least now they were safe.

THE TRICK WITH DRAGONS

A forge as great as the one that Marscal had in mind was no easy feat, yet it was built quickly and to his exacting expectations. It was a forge like no other, and they made it for dragon fire. That was where Geddoe came in.

A native of the Kingdom of Nashoba, his origins were clouded in mystery, but he preferred it that way. His role was to fetch dragons for lords, and that was what he did. The mystery added to his fame, and that added to his price. As dragon hunters and trappers went, Geddoe was one of, if not the best there was, which also added to the price. However, most lords only wanted, or they could only handle and afford, the smaller drakes. Marscal had demanded and paid for something different. He sought after a true, fire-breathing dragon, and that would take more of Geddoe's skill. Still, it wasn't his first ancient dragon hunt. Just the first one that they did not expect him to kill.

He tracked the beast to its lair. The dragon, a green Northern Bristleback, was slumbering for the winter. The perfect time to sneak in and trap it. Geddoe's men followed him inside the cave. His plan was to sneak up on the beast, muzzle it, and then chain it. Best laid plans.

Geddoe had his scarred face wrapped in a tan cloth to help protect him from the dragon's exhaling breath. Though the dragon was asleep and not breathing fire, the breath still had a strong sulfur smell. Following Geddoe's lead, his men had done the same in covering their faces. Years in the dragon hunting trade had engrained these little tips into Geddoe's instincts. However, the dragon's senses were still heightened, even during hibernation.

The hunters crept slowly through the cave, tiptoeing around animal and human bones. A stark reminder of the dangers they were facing.

The chains were stout and made of mithril, a dwarven metal known to be nearly unbreakable. The muzzle was made of the same metal, and that would be the most important part of this plan. Without that muzzle, the dragon could attack with razor-sharp teeth or scorching flames. Geddoe had lost many expert hunters in the past and he was committed to not let that happen again.

The men crept up to the slumbering beast and Geddoe looked at a plump man to his left.

"Now," Geddoe whispered.

The man held up his staff and then slammed the end on the ground, casting a spell that lifted the chains up and over the dragon. Any mage could do simple levitating spells on iron or steel, but mithril, being a metal with magical properties, was harder to control. This mage was truly skilled.

He tapped his staff on the ground again and the chains dropped with a heavy thud on the dragon, waking the beast from its heavy slumber.

The dragon roared, but the chains held the beast down.

"Now Verix!" Geddoe ordered the mage.

Verix lifted his right hand. Three gemstone rings glistened to life. "*Dormi!*" he commanded.

Slowly, the dragon began to lower its head, drifting back to sleep.

"That's the trick with these bastards. Heavy chains and sleep spells," Geddoe grinned. "Okay, let's secure the chains around him and get him loaded onto the ship. We've got a chest full of gold awaiting us."

The men with Geddoe slowly inched their way close to the slumbering beast.

"Get in there and muzzle it!" Geddoe ordered. "With Verix holding the spell, that dragon will sleep for as long as we need."

His men did as they were ordered. Geddoe removed his head, wrapping once the muzzle was in place, and he felt secure that the dragon was asleep again.

"How long will your spell last, anyway?" Geddoe asked Verix.

The mage looked at his boss. "Several hours, at least. I'll cast it again when we get to the ship. I'll have to keep an eye on him. Dragons like this can be tricky."

"As long as it stays asleep while we load him on the cart, then we'll be all set," Geddoe grinned.

The hunters dragged the dragon onto a large cart and dragged it out of the cave.

"Too bad you can't throw a spell to make this trip go any faster," Geddoe said, looking to Verix.

The mage shook his head. "If I do, then the beast will awaken. The two spells will act against each other in a way."

Two hours away, the ship waited, docked in a secluded hamlet away from the key trade routes. It was a smuggling dock to be sure, but the dock had been abandoned in recent years. Too many raids by Knights of the Silver Seal provide fatal to the smuggling business in that area.

Even Geddoe's dragon hunting business suffered. The knights felt that any magical beast was a product of the old gods, and in certain mythologies they were, which meant they needed to be purged from the mortal realm. However, most beasts of the world, including the Ancient and the

Elemental Dragons, existed prior to the teachings of the old gods.

* * * * *

Tsungo walked into the dimly lit room. It was not uncommon for the orc blacksmith to be called into a noble lord's home. He figured it was some custom job. He had done many of those over the years. Tsungo stood in the center of the room. A table sat opposite of him, a few banners hung on the walls, and a few guards stood close by. At the table, Tsungo could make out the silhouettes of those that called him to the stately manor.

"Tsungo, your skills brought you to my attention. My ward, Persa, invited you here because we need a forge. A large forge," Marscal said, sipping a goblet of red wine behind his dining table. "This forge will be used to build a great weapon," Marscal added.

He motioned for an attendant to hand a scroll to Tsungo. The orc looked over the plans. It was indeed a mighty forge. Largest he had ever seen designed, and for fires that would burn hotter than hell itself.

"Is this something that you can build?" Marscal asked.

Tsungo looked at the silhouette that spoke to him. "I think so, yes. It will be daunting, though. I will need a few extra hands."

Marscal stood. He motioned for a couple of other elves, these in chains, to go with Tsungo.

"These lowly stone elves will be your extra hands. You may begin now," Marscal said, sitting back down in his chair.

Tsungo left the room, his new assistants in tow. He wondered where the firepower for such a large forge would come from. He hadn't seen anything quite like that before, but stories did speak of legendary sources. Sources he knew were near impossible to find.

WITHERED GROUND

A few days after meeting up, Nash, Ava, and Cailin set off with Marcus and Venera. They were going to have to make the journey on foot, walking north into a sparsely populated area. The trees were mostly coniferous, and those that weren't had long ago shed their foliage for the winter. The landscape wasn't so bleak, but the cold air reminded the group that the days were growing shorter, as was their time.

Not long into their walk on the third day of travel, they came across a ruined village. The remnants of an attack. Nash and Marcus had their suspicions about might have done the attack.

"The knights just kill with no regard for who they might be attacking. I've seen that in other areas they don't act as extremists, but here they kill anything they see as a threat to humanity," Nash said, as the group walked through the charred village. "At least, their definition of a threat."

He shifted some debris with his foot. Charred bones laid under the rubble. Nash just moved the debris back to where it had been, and he kept walking. He had seen this sort of destruction before. It used to sicken him, but now he was becoming concerned with his growing lack of disgust.

The small village appeared to have been elven before it was reduced to rubble. Some of the runic symbols, who could say how old the symbols were, could still be seen etched on the blackened wood posts. The framed houses held the shape of elven architecture. Often a high, vaulted roof with tile shingles. The fire hadn't touched every building and for what it was worth, that was a blessing.

"When you say other areas, you're talking about the western nations and kingdoms?" Marcus asked.

Nash nodded. "In the west they treat with the mages and even employ some as healers. There is still tension, of course, but the respect is there too."

"That's how you got on with them, the Knights of the Silver Seal?" Ava interjected.

Nash stopped walking through the village. He lowered his head. "I helped some after I left the guild. Just to give them a hand during the Kalihar Succession war," he sighed. "That war was hurting a lot of innocent people, and the knights wanted to stop that. So, I joined a band to help them out. They were a good bunch of knights. I think they went up north to the Sile Empire after the war."

Cailin looked at Nash. "Why did you leave the guild?"

The older mage looked at her. His face showed his annoyance, having answered the question in his mind a million times.

"I left because the last Grand Mage was killed by another mage that was meant to be some sort of savior. He was supposed to usher in a new world for mages. He was going to save the magical world," Nash said sarcastically.

"A lot of the mages liked his ideas too, but he ended up dead, and those of us that didn't follow him felt betrayed at the Grand Mage's murder. We were also betrayed by those that followed him. Braga, that ass, tore the guild apart and didn't even care. He murdered so many and no one that followed him seems to be bothered by it. Like it was some retribution for some made up insult," Nash scoffed. "I left before Sabutai avenged us."

"But Sabutai has helped to rebuild the guild," Cailin replied.

"Yes, he has, and he has done a hell of a job, but the guilds are scorched earth in my and a few others' opinion. The betrayal from within was too great and to be honest, the call of gold from mercenary bands is too great. Let Sabutai rebuild the guilds and prosper, but as for me, I have my own ways of prospering and those ways involve lots of gold."

"A man of my own heart!" Marcus smiled.

Nash gave a chuckle as he began to walk on. "In truth, Cailin, I was a terrible mage. I made a better fighter that could heal myself and my friends at the end of a fight."

"That may come in handy," Ava said.

She knew the value a fighter would have in the coming days if the knights or anything else decided to show up.

Ava looked around and saw the setting sun just above the western horizon. She noted the changing weather and nodded to herself.

"Let's camp here. The clouds rolling in might bring rain and we can still get some shelter from these roofs, though tattered," she said to her companions.

No one seemed to want to contest her opinion on the matter, instead silently agreeing.

They unloaded their packs, while Nash began to gather dry sticks and kindling for the campfire. It didn't take long to start a roaring fire and soon Marcus had a hot stew brewing up in a roasting pot.

"Leeks and carrots will make this a hearty meal," Marcus bragged.

Venera, who had left earlier, returned with three rabbits. Not too big, but just enough meat for the group to be satisfied.

She looked at the others as she began skinning the rabbits. "The knights ran off a lot of the game around here," Venera looked around at her companions. "This land is ancient. Many beasts ran through these hills and plains. Before humans came, the winds would whisper magic in the moonlight."

Cailin looked at Venera. "What sort of magic? I've heard of elementals coming out and even the sort of magic that ancient mages could do."

Venera nodded. "Those ancients still haunt these lands," she motioned around the camp. "They were all over these parts until the guild put them down and forced them to submit. Just like they tried to do to the Quarmi. Now the Knights of the Silver Seal want to put those guild mages down."

"A never-ending cycle." Marcus said.

"Of sorts," Venera agreed. "Mighty were the kings and mages of the days before the fallen came to our world," she finished butchering the rabbit and slid them into the pot. "Our magic was everywhere, and we felt so strong. Our world was brought to heel when the fallen ones brought their sickness to us and made us hate. Our magic became corrupted until the fallen ones were banished," Venera stirred the pot. "Now the only people that talk of such things are crazy folks and old ladies."

"Which are you?" Ava smirked.

"Someone can be both," Venera smiled.

The earlier walking had worn the group and after the meal was finished, everyone but Nash fell asleep. Cailin woke up with the moon high in the sky. Nash saw her moving near the fire.

"Can't sleep?" He asked.

"Not really," Cailin sighed. She moved to sit next to Nash. "It's odd, but I think I can feel what Venera was talking about. The magic surrounding us."

"That's unlikely. The magic that used to be in this land, around the world for that matter, isn't wafting in the air. Not anymore. Now it is all born into us," Nash answered.

Cailin nodded, but she wasn't convinced. "That's what the guild teaches," she frowned. "But what if the guild is wrong?"

"Wouldn't be the first time."

"No, it wouldn't."

Nash gritted his teeth. "You think the guild could be wrong about you?"

Cailin looked at Nash and he could see the optimism in the moon's light reflecting off her eyes.

"Look, I can't say how dark marked mages get those powers, but I can say if the guild tells you anything, either they are half-truths or flat out wrong," Nash said. "But, for the dark mark power, it's pretty much a done deal. You're in a bad spot. There is some hope for you, though. If anyone can help you, it would be Sabutai, but he can't take it away. You are what you are."

"I know," Cailin replied. "That's not what I'm concerned with," she looked off toward the distant mountains. "Mages like me are run out of so many places or we wind up dead. Every knight of the Silver Seal thinks that any mage could be dark marked, so we all should be burned at the stake," she shook her head. "But what if these powers could be used for the benefit of giving life?"

"Life from death?" Nash asked.

"It's a never-ending cycle," Cailin answered. "We come from dirt and go back to dirt only to come back again. I know it's not possible to give life through magic, but what if death isn't the worst of it?"

Nash nodded without replying. He thought about it, and she was right. Life and death were both part of the world and worked in tangent. Where was it written that they had to be against each other?

Nash looked at Cailin. "You should sleep. We have a long day of walking ahead of us."

Cailin smiled and went back to her bedroll. Doubtful that she slept well.

When she did sleep, dreams came to her showing her visions of strange and wicked things. A kingdom by the sea, a pair of lovers, wicked men, and women. All shadowed by a red moon. She saw a sea of fog and a faint green light in the distance through the fog. Sometimes bars, chains and shackles would wrap around beasts or other more sinister looking creatures.

That night, as she slept, the shadow turned into a man. Hooded and mysterious. He watched her, spoke in some weird sounding tongue, and beckoned her to him. She tried to move away but his pull was too strong. She couldn't resist him. It took all her strength to pull herself out of the dream. Another nightmare, another morning of waking up panting while everyone else seemed fine. Normal.

Once she was awake and everyone was ready to journey, the group was off walking to the north. It was imperative that they reached the Reposo before the early season snowfalls. That was only a couple of weeks away. The journey to the north was quicker over the next few days. Whether it was their haste, for wanting to be away from the burned village, or something else pushing them on, it didn't matter. They were moving and days ahead of their new schedule.

The countryside posed little obstacle for the group. Rolling hills that backed up to a thick forest along the eastern border. The trail would take the party to Montrah, and from there they would charter a boat to take them to the mall port town of Reposo. The journey was picturesque and, while easy, they kept looking over their shoulder for signs of anyone following them.

After a few days, however, things took an unfortunate turn. Cailin walked alongside her companions, but she was feeling heavy with each step. Something was pulling at her from beneath her, around her, and behind her. Cailin knew something was trying to hold her and keep her from moving forward.

"Wait, stop!" Cailin called out to the group.

The others turned to see her.

"What's the matter?" Ava asked.

"Something... a shadow is holding me," Cailin said. Her voice sounding softer than ever. "It has darkened each step I've taken."

Cailin tried to move, but her feet were planted, as if rooted into the ground.

"There is an evil presence here," Venera said. The elf looked around, drawing her kukri from her belt. "Be mindful of spirits."

Ava looked around. "And that blade will stop them?"

Venera slashed the blade along her hand, opening a gash and coating her knife with blood. "It will now."

Ava raised an eyebrow. "Alright then."

Nash and Marcus walked to their group.

"Whatever is holding Cailin is trying to keep us from something," Nash said.

"Can magic do that?" Ava asked.

"Not usually," Cailin said. "But this feels different."

Suddenly, the group heard a horrific screech coming from the tree line. The group turned to the noise. A form lifted from the forest. It rose high into the sky, concealing itself in the rays of the sun.

"That's not a good sign," Nash said. He turned to the others. "We need to run now!"

"I can't!" Cailin yelled as another piercing screech rang out.

Nash rushed to the Cailin, grabbing her by the waist. He pulled up, trying to pick the young woman up, but she wouldn't move.

"Damn!"

Marcus ran over to help, but even with the extra strength, both the men were unsuccessful.

"Here it comes!" Ava called out, pulling her blade out.

Cailin looked up as the dark form approached. She squinted, trying to see the creature, blinded by the sunlight.

"Can't be!" Cailin said.

"What?" Asked Nash.

Cailin gasped. "A harpy."

The group looked up as the winged beast dove down upon them.

Cailin recognized the path the harpy was flying and pushed Nash out of the way just as the harpy attacked. The creature rose again, missing its prey.

Cailin whispered an incantation, inching slowly to freedom with each word uttered. Just as the harpy turned for a second attack, Cailin freed herself from the force holding her. She planted her feet firmly, raised her hand, and a flash of light erupted from her palm, directed at the harpy. The beast flailed from the magical attack. Its body was prone above the ground.

"Let's see if you like being stuck in one place," Cailin taunted.

She whispered another spell, freezing the harpy in midair.

Ava spotted the beast at a low enough height for her daggers. She threw them with expert precision, hitting the harpy twice in the chest. Cailin released her attack, and the harpy fell to the ground.

Venera walked over and kicked at the beast's ribs.

"It's dead," the elf said.

Nash walked over to it. "Too bad," he said with an eye to Ava. "We could have tried to get some information."

Ava rolled her eyes. "I'm an assassin, not a city guard. I'm not hired to collect information. I'm hired to collect bodies."

"We can still get some information," Cailin said, walking up to the harpy.

Nash nodded. "Is there still time?"

"Most scholars think that the brain has about ten minutes of activity before it truly dies. So, maybe," Cailin said.

She knelt next to the harpy's head and touched the beast's forehead. The orange gemstone on her bracelet glowed as Cailin's eyes rolled back into her head. Soon she was mumbling in an incoherent tongue.

"The language of the fallen ones," Venera said. "Harpies are the unholy offspring of Ren and Malum. Two of the worst old gods or fallen ones."

In an instant, Cailin was back among the living.

"This isn't good," she said, looking at the others. She steadied herself on the ground, one hand on her knee. "This one is the lookout. The others are on the far side of those trees. Feasting in a small village."

"Feasting? On flesh?" Ava asked.

Cailin nodded.

Nash looked to the trees. "How many more?"

"Six."

"We have to save the village!" Venera growled.

Marcus shook his head. "Probably not the best idea."

"But if those people need help..."

Cailin stood up. "It took most of my energy to cast that spell on this harpy and then enter her mind. I can't do it six more times. Maybe once more, but I'm not sure."

"Unless your elf blood blade can kill six harpies at once, we need to run and finish the mission," Ava said, gathering her pack that had fallen on the ground.

Venera cursed. "It could, but I can't go alone. If everyone wants to run, then we run," she said before sheathing her blade.

"Might need to tell me how your blood works," Ava said. "Later."

The group rushed off to the east, retreating away from the village. Soon, a light was flaring up from behind the forest. Nash noticed it from the hilltop vantage point.

"Poor fools think that fire will help," Nash said.

"Or someone is covering the place up," Marcus responded.

Nash raised an eyebrow. "Come to think of it, I've never heard stories of harpies burning villages," Nash replied. He looked at Marcus. "You think they have some help?"

Marcus shrugged. "That fire didn't start until we got closer to these hills. By that time, several hours had passed since our own attack. Someone doesn't want the harpy attack to be known."

"Then the town from the other day could have met the same fate?" Ava asked, walking up to the pair.

Nash nodded. "Perhaps," he sighed. "How is Cailin?"

Ava shrugged. "Fine, I guess. She still says that she feels some sort of presence or shadow around her. Something pulling her from within," she motioned with her head toward Venera sitting by the campsite. "The elf is watching her."

"The elf has a name," Marcus said, his eyes narrowing with a scowl.

"Yea, and a large knife. Those stone elves are thieves and cutthroats. Got to keep an eye on her or just send her away. The latter would be best."

"High and mighty for an assassin," Marcus retorted.

"I get paid to kill. Stone elves do it for lust."

Nash shook his head. "Rumors and propaganda to stir division among the elves and other mortals."

"Believe it or not, some of those rumors aren't true," Marcus said with a huff.

"Whatever. She covered her blade in blood, and that's a deadly magic I don't want any part of," Ava scoffed. "If she tries to knife us, I won't say I told you so, but believe me, I'll be thinking it," Ava smirked before walking back to the campfire.

Cailin enjoyed a glass of wine. Several glasses, actually. She couldn't place her fear or feelings. Her knee was shaking, bouncing up and down. Venera chalked it up to nerves, but Cailin felt something different.

Not only was she feeling a nervous energy, but something pulled at her still. Something that felt odd or dark. She couldn't figure it out. Her mind was racing with a ton of what ifs.

Cailin could not figure it out. The feeling, the pull, or the events with the harpy. Something didn't feel right, but everything looked... okay. And that tore her up from the inside out. What was worse was that she wasn't sure she could even tell anyone anything about it. Would they understand, or would they want to get rid of her for being a dark-marked mage? Was this part of being dark marked?

Cailin couldn't begin to even answer these questions.

WHAT LIES WITHIN

Nothing prepares anyone for working with a dragon. Their large, rather difficult to get close to without angering, and most breathe some sort of flame. Red, blue, green, or any other color of flame. It made little difference because it would kill. Geddoe, however, jumped at the chance to wrangle any dragonkin beast. He even had some experience with the dracosapians.

Those were the beastfolk that had descended from dragons eons before. At the very least, Geddoe was a dragon hunter, but in reality, he was a dragon scholar.

This dragon, however, was different.

Brutish and full of rage, that even surprised the experienced dragon hunter. Eleven men had already lost their lives to the best, and now Geddoe's loyal second in command, Verix, was in a trancelike state against it. The spell that Verix had used to bind the dragon to sleep was causing Verix to be taken over mentally. In a last-ditch effort to defend himself, the mage had countered the dragon's spell with another, locking both within Verix's mind.

Geddoe had taken residence in an abandoned castle. The exterior crumbling around them. He knew he would be late on the delivery, but his second in command, his friend, was more important than the delivery.

Geddoe was sitting beside his friend's bed in a dank, dark room when he heard footsteps behind him. Amasis and Lestrade walked into the room.

"We certainly weren't expecting to get your message, but it's fortunate that we did," Amasis said to Geddoe, taking a seat next to him.

Geddoe tried to smile. "Verix thought you'd appreciate hearing what that explorer found."

Lestrade put her hand on Geddoe's shoulder. "He'll wake up."

"I don't know. He's trying to fight that dragon. It's a powerful beast without magic, but this one..." He paused. "This one is the strongest I've ever come across," Geddoe sighed. "We were lucky to get the beast under control and find this castle to hold on in."

Amasis looked around the room. "A dusty and dank old fortress but one with lots of history," he stood up. "Do you know anything about this place?"

Geddoe shook his head, as did Lestrade.

"This is the ancestral home of the Inquisitor Kings," Amasis said.

"The Inquisitor Kings? Who were they?" Geddoe asked.

Lestrade frowned. "Them I do know about. They were evil heretic kings.

Followers of a religion that was an amalgamation of the old gods and the Faith of the Cavern Gods. They ruled large swathes of land nearly a thousand years ago. Human sacrifice was their preferred method to maintain control and to appease their gods."

"And then one day, their kingdom, this castle, burned. All in one fell swoop," Amasis finished.

"I could see the worn stone had damage," Geddoe replied. He stood up and walked to the far wall, placing a hand over the cool stone. "You think this is not by chance?"

Lestrade shook her head. "Nothing is by chance. Not you stopping here, the messenger, and the solution," she removed a scroll from her pouch. "We need a flayer to rescue Verix if he can't defeat the dragon's will on his own, and there just happens to be one travelling to Reposo by way of Montrah."

"Montrah is a day's ride," Geddoe said. "How do you know this? How do you know that there is a flayer heading that way?"

"A birdie told us," Amasis frowned. "For a steep price, I might add."

"Fatima?" Geddoe asked.

"We all have the same contact, it seems." Lestrade smirked. "She's had contact with Nash. They are working some angle with the Shrouded Guild, and it is dealing with the animal attacks."

"What do you two have to do with them?"

Amasis sighed. "Lestrade picked up your message about the Fallen Kingdom and we're investigating that. It seems our paths have crossed."

"We were hired to bring back an eternal dragon. It has now corrupted my friend," Geddoe replied. "Is that something that concerns your quest?"

"Perhaps," Lestrade said. "If this flayer is needed to revive Verix and perhaps see what the dragon's fate holds, then yes."

"Truth is, we don't even know for sure yet," Amasis replied.

Geddoe nodded. "No matter. I'll send my men to retrieve this flayer and we'll figure it out from there."

"No," Amasis said, holding up his hand. "We must go and get her. Just us three."

Geddoe looked at the mage inquisitively. "Why us three?"

Lestrade grinned. "A prophecy?"

"Really?" Geddoe asked.

"No," Lestrade smirked. "Of course, not. It's because they are Shrouded Guild with a Blackbird ally. That means whatever they are doing is meant to be secret. I don't wish to run either of those groups afoul, therefore, we tread cautiously and respectfully."

"We aren't simply getting the flayer and bringing her back here," Amasis added. "We are going to probably need to make a deal. Possibly to aid them in some way."

"Fine," Geddoe said. "Whatever we have to do, let's get to it."

* * * * *

Cailin walked along the grown over path. It was an old smuggling route that Marcus had used in the past. Her mind still swirled with thoughts from the harpy's mind. There were darker images that she couldn't shake. Something was still pulling at her and with the images in her head, that pull was even stronger. She heard voices within the harpy's mind. Voices that all repeated the same phrase.

Mors, e sono non chegará á vinganza. Uma vez que a halve maen sobe, la Regina Mortis acordará,[1] Cailin whispered over and over to herself.

---

[1] Death, and sleep will not stem to coming revenge. Once the half-moon rises, the Queen of Death will awake

"What was that?" Venera asked, hearing Cailin's soft whisper.

Cailin startled out of her haze, shaking her head. "Yeah, just thinking about something from earlier."

"From the attack?"

Cailin didn't respond, but her mouth twitched at the edges.

"Hmm. It won't do well to dwell on the harpy," Venera said, catching on to Cailin's expression. "They can feel the fear you give them."

"I'm not afraid of them," Cailin said defiantly.

Venera sneered. "You should be."

Cailin tried to put it out of her mind, but the thoughts got worse with each passing day. The strange pull gripped ever tighter; her own voice was becoming more drowned out as she tried to collect her thought each day. Worse were the dreams each night. Visions from attacked villages, and images from the harpy's memories. The lust of her kills. Most were for sport.

Cailin closed her eyes, and she saw the same face. Half of the face was that of a beautiful woman. Majestic and fair. Auburn hair flowed down past her shoulders, silky and radiant. An artist would never find difficulty painting such beauty, not from that half.

The other half was something more grotesque. A skull, rotted and worn from time. The eye socket was empty and black. The two lines of teeth within the jawbones were worn and cracked. This was the face of a demon.

Cailin looked at this woman, half in life and half in death, her voice mocking her in two tones. When the woman spoke, the echo of a disembodied voice rang deep in Cailin's ears. It spoke to her and her fears. She saw it in each face of every person who was in her dreams. She heard the voice speaking other's words. In their faces, during her waking hours. Behind their eyes, she saw the emptiness of the skull's eye socket.

It was like that for days, repeating words in other tongues, in her own. Words of twisted horror, and manipulation. Soon, another voice began to speak, intertwined, and mingled with each other. Another woman spoke.

The darkness is the cure. Your mind is fading. Entering into such magic will erode away what little sanity you have left. Accept Muerta's help and reach into her power. Only then will you find peace.

Those words pulled at her as if she felt a comfort with the idea of giving in. Something about the voice felt like a mother's warmth during a thunderstorm. She had not known much love or comfort like that in her youth. Hardstone barony was a tough place to live for those born under the dark mark, and Cailin's mother abandoned her to the guild as a child. Only the handmaids of the guild were there to dry her tears. Few would, however.

Cailin shook her head whenever she felt herself begin to slip into the words' trance. She wondered; could the others sense it in her? Could they hear it too? Who is it? Is it one of them?

The group kept walking on along the trail. It was a bit overgrown, but still passable. She looked to the path, some dirt caking up from recent rains, but the grass was still lush even in the colder temperatures. The trees along the path were mostly pine, conifers, which would still be green through the winter months. Large and imposing, these trees felt different to the young mage.

Nash, scouting ahead, stopped a short distance away from the rest of the group. He motioned for Ava to join him. Cailin watched as the pair talked. A chill went down her spine. She could feel the faded presence of life not far away. It was faint, but she could feel the emotions of the dead nearby.

"You see their mouths moving. You know what they are saying," a voice in her head spoke.

"It's not good," another voice answered.

"Shut up," Cailin whispered.

Nash walked into the forest and disappeared among the trees while Ava motioned for the others to join her.

"Nash saw some movement just past the trees. He is going to check it out," Ava said.

Before anyone could respond, Nash reappeared. He motioned his head toward the trees behind them.

"Come see this," he said.

The group walked over and into the forest. A short distance away, they found the movement that Nash had noticed. Hanging from several large branches were thirteen villagers. Five men, four women, and four children.

"They haven't been here long. The blood from the mouths still has some shine to it," Ava said.

Marcus touched one of the men's legs. "This one is cold. A day since they were killed, probably."

Cailin stayed back from the group. She saw the bodies hanging, but she didn't want to look up at their faces.

Nash looked to Cailin. "Do you think that you can get anything from their memories?"

"They want to use you," a voice in Cailin's mind said.

Cailin squinted and turned her head away, looking at the ground.

"He needs your power and yet he fears it," the second voice said.

"He will kill you eventually," a third, new voice spoke. *"Because of his fear. It will drive him to murder."*

"Cailin?" Nash said. The others looked at her.

Cailin was shaking her head at the words of the voices.

Nash saw she wasn't hearing him. "Cailin!"

She snapped her head up and looked at him. Her eyes were wide. "I'm sorry, I didn't hear you," she lied.

Nash sighed. "Can you read their memories?"

She shook her head. "No, they are too long dead."

"Can you try?" Nash asked.

"No!" Cailin yelled in frustration. "No, I won't invade any more dead minds!" she rushed out of the forest.

"Cailin!" Nash yelled.

"Leave her," Ava said. "I'll go get her," Ava followed her path out to catch up with Cailin.

Marcus looked at Venera. "Let's get these bodies down."

"No," Nash stopped them. "We can't leave evidence that we were here. Leave them."

Venera looked at Nash with a grimace. Marcus just nodded and turned away.

Nash looked around the area for any tracks. "We need to make sure that we aren't going to be followed."

"Or that we aren't following something deadlier than us," Marcus added.

Nash nodded.

Soon the trio had rejoined Cailin and Ava. Cailin was silent and sullen, sitting on the ground, tears streaming from her eyes. Ava stood over her. She wasn't trying to comfort her. Doubtful that she would know how.

"Let's move," Nash said. He offered a hand to Cailin. She took his hand and stood up. He tightened his grip. "We need you to be on your game. Fuck around like that again and we'll send you home," he let her go and started back on the path. "You don't have to read minds or anything if you don't want to, but this is the real world. Death is constant. The guild can't protect you out here. Get your shit together or go home," he finished, his back turned, and walking off toward the north.

"He hates you," a voice in Cailin's head spoke.

"Shut up," Cailin whispered.

Ava looked back at Cailin. She turned back to the path and walked up to Nash.

"Something is going on with Cailin," Ava said.

"Yeah," Nash nodded. "It's the dark mark. The more she uses the powers of dark magic, the more it will try to corrupt her."

"I didn't think magic was like that."

"Elemental magic isn't," Nash replied. "Dark magic and blood magic invites demons and spirits. It comes from demons. At least if you believe the old legends."

"Do you?" Ava asked.

Nash shrugged. "Not sure. Seeing her talk to herself like that makes me wonder, though. She might be hearing voices of demons or spirits. That's what the old legends always spoke of. Venera said that spirits were around this area, so maybe Cailin could be feeling them," Nash glanced behind him to see Cailin.

He looked back at Ava. "I'd like to think she is just having self-doubts, but this feels weird. Did Hitomi mention anything to you about her having these traits?"

"Not at all. She just said that her magic would be useful," Ava sighed. "Hitomi is all about the need-to-know mentality."

"Yea, and yet this seems like something we'd need to know," Nash responded.

"Do you think Hitomi knows?"

Nash shrugged. "Couldn't say for sure, but I would say no as a guess. If she is hearing voices, then that's a distraction we do not need."

* * * * *

Tsungo breathed a sigh of relief. The forge, which had taken a month to piece together, was finished. A monumental task that took every waking hour was done. The construction also took the lives of several of the elf workers. Tsungo figured they were hired on, but their careless use by this cult like group made him question that.

The orc blacksmith walked the corridors, looking for his employer. He turned a corner, a sparkle of light catching his eye. Tsungo walked into the room, dazzling artifacts were displayed along the walls. He picked one up and studied its markings.

"An interesting piece," a voice said from behind Tsungo.

Tsungo turned and saw Marscal standing at the room's entrance. It was the elf he had been searching for.

"Yes, it is," Tsungo said, placing it back on the pedestal.

The tall orc towered over the elderly elf, but he felt uneasy near him. Tsungo tried to make eye contact, but he was having trouble holding to it. Something about the elder elf was off, and a little bit frightening.

"It is an ancient reliquary. We use them to hold the spirits of vanquished foes. That one was an enemy from a couple of centuries ago. Her name was Loreley, a witch from the nameless wastes," Marscal said with a wicked grin.

Tsungo nodded. "I..."

"Of course, you're not here to hear our history. An update perhaps?"

"Oh yes, sir," Tsungo said, relieved he wouldn't have to speak about a statue with a soul trapped inside. "The forge is complete, ready to be lit."

Marscal grinned. He reached out and picked up another small statue. Another reliquary.

"Just in time, I'd say. Our hunter is on his way with the dragon. Soon, he will be able to complete his work," Marscal said.

Tsungo looked confused. "Will you be needing me to forge anything for you?"

Marscal shook his head. "No, my master will need to do the forging himself. It is a special weapon that only he has the skillset and recipe for. However, you will be needed for something else," Marscal pull a small stone jar from his pouch. "This reliquary is empty."

"Is that for the dragon's spirit?" Tsungo asked.

"No," Marscal said with a toothy grin. "It is not."

Marscal grabbed Tsungo's left shoulder tightly. The orc was frozen. He felt a strange sensation running through his body. It was painful. He buckled over. He could see the room change, the color faded from around him, and his vision grew dark. Voices surrounded him, screams and wails of anguish. It was an unnatural feeling, and the sounds scared him. The worst part, besides the pain, was the pitch-black darkness.

Soon it all ended. Tsungo dropped to a heap of dead flesh onto the stone floor.

Marscal turned to an attendant close by. "Make sure that this body is disposed of," he said, placing the now full reliquary back on the wall shelf.

Marscal stepped over the orc's lifeless body and went about his tasks, thankful and excited to get his grand plan in motion.

DARK WHISPERS

Geddoe, Lestrade, and Amasis made their way along the old smugglers' path. They had the information that Marcus was leading the group on the same path heading north. Geddoe and his companions walked south. They had to meet with Nash and Ava, and particularly Cailin.

"If we follow this path, we're bound to intercept them," Amasis said.

"Is there any danger in meeting them?" Lestrade asked. She was a bit more apprehensive. "They have an assassin with them."

"Yeah, and they are on the same side. At least they will be when we introduce ourselves," Amasis replied.

Amasis was leading with the hope that Nash and his companions were willing to help out fellow scholars. Amasis held private concerns, however. He knew Nash from years prior and had an idea that Nash wasn't always open to helping others in dire situations.

Add to the fact that Geddoe was working with others from another guild. One that wanted dragon blood. That would put him in a precarious position. Dragon's blood was not a common ingredient in most magical spells. It was typically reserved for darker magic. If anyone were to question him, then that would certainly make him look less friendly to those working alongside dark marked mage.

Geddoe kept the true extent of his employment silent. Amasis and Lestrade knew he was transporting a dragon. However, they were under the impression that it was for some rich benefactor that wanted an exotic pet.

Within the shadows, shapes followed them. Amasis could feel another presence, but kept it quiet amongst his companions. Better to keep a fast pace than to slow everyone down with fears of something close by. Especially when that something had yet to make itself an enemy of the group. Lestrade could feel Amasis' trepidation, however, yet she didn't let on. She trusted her partner and knew him long enough to know he'd never let her come to harm.

"We aren't far," Geddoe said. "There is a village nearby along the smugglers' route that they will probably stop at. We can rest there and wait."

"If they already stopped off there and left?" Lestrade asked.

"Then we would have seen them," Geddoe responded curtly.

"Could they have gone another path?" Amasis asked, understanding Lestrade's question.

Geddoe stopped walking and turned to the others.

He sighed before speaking his mind. "Let's hope not. This land isn't a friendly place for humans right now," he said. "Besides, if they did break away from this path, then we'd have a hard time tracking them in such an area."

Amasis raised an eyebrow. "Aren't you the world's greatest dragon tracker? Humans would pose a problem?"

"Dragons are big and leave very noticeable signs. It doesn't take a lot of skill to track them. Bringing them down is the hard part," Geddoe replied. "Humans, that's tougher because when a human doesn't want to be found, they can hide a lot easier."

"Noted," Amasis said.

Geddoe turned around and led the group south along the path. He thought of the preceding conversation. *Dragons were easier*, he thought. *Much easier.* They required skill and strength, of course, but in the end, a dragon would act as a dragon. Sure, if the legends were true, some had a high level of intelligence, ranging from speech and comprehension. Yet, they were still dragons and instincts always took over.

Humans were the contradictions.

Only humans would shake hands with their right, and then use the left hand to stab that same person in the back.

Maybe other mortal races did the same. Geddoe thought of it all. The deviousness of humanity and its penchant for betrayal. Almost like it was instinct. Maybe humans were as simple as dragons. Maybe humans also acted on instinct, just a less honorable one.

The natural state of being for humans was to conquer. The natural state of elves was to control. The natural state of dwarves was to bend things to their will. For the Quarmi, it was to subvert the existence of magic to their own lives. Geddoe considered these theories of lives. He had felt the scorn of humanity's notion of kill or be killed. He knew firsthand the deadliness of the shortest-lived mortal race, and yet he saw the irony in their strongest desire, legacy.

Geddoe had been born to a poverty-stricken family, the eighth child of a dirt farmer. His father was killed in some noble lord's war when the young Geddoe was still a toddler. His mother was forced to sell several of her children to others, for whatever purpose, who knows and more than likely for nothing pleasant. Yet, Geddoe was a survivor. He ran away when he was strong enough, killing one of his captors and staking out on his own. He traveled the world, fighting and kill for the highest bidder, until he realized he could make a more lucrative life for himself hunting dangerous creatures. If he succeeded, then he would get rich, temporarily at least. He never learned how to properly save money since he never had any to save. However, if he died hunting some beast, then it didn't matter much in the end. That was the way for humans. Hunt and kill until you die, either by someone's blade or nature's doing. Either way, death was the only constant. That and pain. With humans, there was never any mercy. War, poverty, death. Nothing else, at least not in Geddoe's eyes.

* * * * *

Nash sat next to a campfire across from Cailin. She eyed the man much more carefully than she had before. Whether it was the voices, or her own intuition, she wasn't sure. She looked and saw a glint of metal bouncing on Nash's chest. She squinted, trying to make out the image. Finally, Cailin gave up and asked.

"What's that you're wearing around your neck, Nash?" Cailin asked.

Nash shook himself from his trance, watching the fire, and gripped at his medallion.

"This?" he said with a smirked. "This is just an old fire emblem from my mother. She gave it to me when I joined the guild," she chuckled. "It was meant to protect me. It had a Carnelian stone in it once."

"What happened to it?"

Nash sighed. "I sold it for booze some years back."

Cailin nodded. She might have been fresh out of the guild, but she knew that life was difficult for mages in many parts of the world.

"We might have a few more gemstones in the guild stores. We can refit one when we get back."

Nash gave her a half-smile. "It's okay. I kind of like it like this. Reminds me of how far I've come since leaving the guild," he sighed. "The guy I sold it to probably wanted it for better performance in bed," Nash chuckled. "That's what most people use those stones for."

"That and bravery," Cailin added.

Nash nodded. "Bravery, I sure showed that."

Cailin bit her tongue. She wanted to comfort him, but something stopped her.

"It's no matter. Life worked out well enough. Fate I guess," Nash added.

Cailin nodded with her own half-smile. "In my homeland they say your fate is already decided, plucked from the threads of the gods. No matter what, your life is all planned out by divine beings," she picked up a small twig and tossed it into the fire. "I guess that makes it easy for the people back home to be brave. Easier said than done."

Nash noted Cailin's expression. Her feigned smile had dissolved from her face. She looked tired and worn. The road can make the finest silks look ragged in mere hours, but Cailin looked different. Her demure was worn and wretched. Something was hiding behind her green tented eyes.

"Are you doing okay with everything?" Nash asked. His voice was like that of a parent or an older sibling comforting a child. "You know, with..." he pointed to his head.

"My mind?" Cailin asked. "No, maybe. I don't know really," she looked around her before turning back to the fire. "I see things. Black spots or flecks flying around. Sometimes they're white spots. I see them when I turn my eyes. They make me think something is there when it's not or when no one else sees them. I'm tired and losing sleep. I just don't feel myself, but then again, I'm not sure I ever did."

"Those things you see, maybe just anxiety? Nervous about your first mission?"

Cailin gave a halfhearted nod. "I thought about that. I have this small rash too. Kind of a thing with stress, I've been told. Did you or Ava get like this your first time?"

Nash tilted his head back and cracked a soft smile. "No, but I was already a battle veteran by that time," he said, then he looked at Cailin's forlorn face and continued. "My first battle, though, my stomach was in knots. I know some of the others were feeling nerves too, all in different ways," he sighed. "What you're feeling might be stress and nerves, but I'm not a doctor. Everyone might feel stress in vastly different ways."

Cailin nodded. "Thanks."

"Sorry, I wish I could be more help."

Cailin looked at Nash with a smile. "No, you've been very helpful. Thank you, Nash."

"But you still seem down."

"I guess that after all these years of feeling different, I just wanted to have something about what's going on in my life to be normal," Cailin mused.

"Normal is overrated," a voice from behind Cailin said.

Cailin turn and saw Ava coming to sit next to her.

"Normal is just a word people use to put other people in cages. Physically and mentally. When you break from the herd, you die, or you become greater than the herd. Those in power don't want the latter to happen, so they tell people that you're not normal when you're just growing beyond what they want you to be. Fuck them and fuck normal," Ava finished.

"Eloquent," Nash scoffed. He stood up. "Try to get some rest, Cailin. I noticed that you didn't eat much today."

"I wasn't really feeling hungry," Cailin replied.

Nash nodded. "Well, rest then. It will be a long day tomorrow and a lot of walking before we reach the village." He looked at Ava before walking off. "You too."

Ava waved the man off as he turned from the fire.

* * * * *

Persa walked up a lone mound, far past Tyranos. It was a place revered for centuries as a tomb. A great beast, or warrior, was buried beneath the rocks and sands. No one could remember the occupant, but all knew the legends. Curses, mysterious lights, and other such nonsense kept all away.

Not Persa, though. She had a purpose for being there. She made her way to the top of the mound, approaching a figure standing at the summit. A man, alone, hooded, and dangerous. Persa could feel the man's power. A dark aura wafted around him, something strong, old, and evil. His smell was even evil. A mixture of sulfur, brimstone, and burning leaves.

"This spot is where they buried the elder dragon Atash Teresnak," the man said as Persa walked up behind him. He never turned to regard her. "He ravaged these lands eons ago, yet his cult lived until the days of my youth. In my final mortal moment, I spoke to him, praying that he would grant me life eternal."

The man held out his arm. The cloak shifted, and revealed shriveled skin on a boney hand. He clenched his fist.

"That prayer was granted," he said with a cackle. "For a price. One I am willing to pay."

The man turned to Persa, and she dropped to the ground on her knees.

"Now I walk this land, healing, regaining strength," he continued. "Feeling the power around me, yet beyond my reach. Soon, though, Atash Teresnak will grant me sight beyond this plane. Sight withheld by the usurpers of the power that we crave," he touched Persa's bowed head. "Rise my friend."

Persa did as commanded. "My lord," she smiled. "The forge is near completion."

The man smiled. "Good. Once it is complete, I can enter the flames and regain the power that was lost. I can forge the weapon that will serve our needs."

"Balt the Blessed will return," Persa grinned.

"Blessed? Lies to cover the truth. Always such a human way," Balt shook his head. "Yes, Balt will be reborn. Years spent in the abyss, searching for truth, asleep to the world, dead to others. Balt is who will be reborn, but not the blessed. Not the lie of humanity. No, Balt the Devourer of the World will be born!"

Persa grinned. "My lord, Balt, we shall all rejoice at the coming of the new world, devoid of mortal pain. Yet, Geddoe has yet to bring the elder dragon."

Balt smiled, running his hand gently over Persa's brown skin cheek.

"That isn't the plan. A decoy for those we must cleanse from our ranks," Balt retracted his hand. "No, the true source of the flame will be here."

Balt raised his arms, extending his hands out.

Persa looked around and noticed the ground trembling around her.

"Rise great terror, and walk with your loyal followers," Balt's voice echoed across the plane.

The ground beneath the pair thundered and shuddered before cracking around them. Cracks and fissures grew as dust, sand, and smoke rose from deep within the earth. A red light glowed from beneath the rocks and a roar echoed around the pair. A bone hand appeared, and then part of a wing, until the dragon's

head knocked stones and sand away. It let out a loud roar. Balt smiled.

"Come, my old friend, let's rejoin the land of the living," he grinned wickedly.

* * * * *

It was a heavy burden, the thought of what will happen next. Living in a world where no one knew from one day to the other, one hour to the other, what their lives would hold. Cailin's homeland in Hardstone, within the Kingdom of Lotcala, said that the gods held your life in their hands eons before you were born. A fate unchanging and decided like thread in a loom for a marvelous tapestry. A similar mythology held by other cultures in the world.

Still, others spoke of different destinies. Darker destinies, intertwined with the ebb and flow of the unseen universe around mortality.

Whatever the case, for Cailin it was hell. Each step was a step into an unknown. Perhaps one moment she was feeling better, secure, and confident, but at the slightest thought, it could change. Her entire demeanor would alter to fit this fresh fear. A fear that she had never felt before, but that was now as powerful as anything she could imagine. No amount of logic could dispel the fear in her mind. Sharp, stabbing pains gnawed at her physically. Her back, her shoulders, and her neck. She'd feel jabs and pricks piercing her skin, but when she'd look, there was nothing there. Cailin would ask one of the others if they could see anything, but nothing was ever there. Venera would try to comfort her, but that did little good in Cailin's increasingly rattled mind.

She often wondered if any of it was real, or just in her head.

Were there people walking alongside them unseen? She didn't know. Did she see movement, hear voices? She wasn't sure. Cailin would wake up from a noise in the dead of night, but none of her companions would be roused. Was the noise even physical? Was it the magic driving her insane like it did so to many other mages before her? Could it be nothing? Her own fear of the powers she was born with?

Cailin knew the old tales well enough. The other students in the guild would taunt her. Frighten her about her ultimate fate one day. Those tales and taunts all ended the same, with Cailin slowly going mad because of the magic within her. This wasn't like elemental magic, nor was it useful, functional magic. It was dark magic. It was a form of magic that brought death and misery. It defiled the life of the mortal world. This was a cursed life, and everyone knew it. Whether they said anything about it was another matter.

She could remember her mother cursing the old stories, and silently Cailin. Or did those memories of her mother lie? She remembered a loving mother, but did she make up the idea of her mother's secret hate for her? Did she curse Cailin or the magic?

What made dark magic so terrible? Isn't it only a name?

Cailin wondered this at length. Now, while she is walking to some little village in the middle of nowhere, along a smuggler's path, it was a good time to ponder the thought.

Since the beginning of recorded time, there were mages that could perform many great feats of magic. Maybe the first mages were shunned or feared. Perhaps even hated. It must have been something wondrous to see the first mages weave spectacular images and conjure great multitudes of effects around the mortal world. Yet, she had to think about those that held the power to kill. A power to drain life, to wander into someone's dreams and thoughts.

Cailin, like other dark-marked mages, could torment someone's mind if she wanted to. All she had to do was enter it, but she didn't like to do it. She hated the feeling of being within someone else's mind. Unfortunately, it wasn't always voluntary for the mage. It was never voluntary for the victim. She would do anything to keep herself from entering someone's mind. She wished she could protect others as well, but that wasn't an option. The power within her was daunting, all magic was. However, this was a power that corrupted all who used it.

Cailin knew her time was limited. It always was for people like her. Mages like her. The magic burned a hole inside of them. The voices started first, usually after using the dark magic. Not just using like draining life from houseplants, but rather from purposeful use. Something like voluntarily entering another being's mind. Opening that door will only lead you astray.

At least, that is what Cailin had always heard.

She had opened that doorway and now the voices grew louder. Whispers at first. Maybe they had been there ever since she could remember, but now they were walking beside her. Just not really there, but present. Then she'd use more magic, maybe trying to help or to stop something worse from happening.

Cailin would use her magic to help the world from being destroyed. All good intentions, but Cailin knew that the path to hell was paved with good intentions. She would just succumb to the darkness. It would take her like it had taken so many before her. She would wind up in hell, even before her own death, most likely by her own hand. She'd live in a hell that she created. It was her fate. It was the fate of every dark-marked mage. Ever since the day of her birth, she has been marked to kill others and then die.

Visions would continue. What were they? Cailin wondered this to a distraction. More than those dark spots, but people. Were they from her entering the harpy's mind? Is that what the harpy had seen? A woman, half dead and half alive. Dark visions, torture, and death. So much death. An old man. The visions were never clear, but that didn't mean she didn't fear them. All of the visions, except the old man, spoke to her in another language. It was guttural and hard to make out. She knew a few other languages, but this one was strange to her. The old man just smiled. She thought it was a smile. Cailin wasn't sure if she wanted it to be a smile or not.

One other vision bothered her. It plagued her. A prison, not of stone or steel, but magic. Was it the veil? Something stirred behind it. It too, spoke the strange dialect Cailin couldn't understand. Something evil, that much she could feel. She couldn't understand it, but it too called out to her. What it wanted; she couldn't say, but she knew that she wanted to stay as far from it as she could.

She walked along the path with the others. She could see the flickers of movement, catching her eye and drawing her attention. They were in every direction.

DREAMS OF ANOTHER SHORE

Shadowy figures invaded her every dream. No sleep was restful. Each night, Cailin rose from slumber more than once, sweating and panting from a terrible nightmare. Glimpses of something beyond her own world. Beyond the world that everyone was in. Was there more? Was there another plane?

Cailin couldn't fathom it.

She dreamt of lost cities, burnt to ash, covered in suffocating sand. Ships at the bottom of the ocean, swimming through a maelstrom of drowned corpses. She tried each night to think of pleasant visions, attempting to stop the nightmares. All in vain. There was no peace for the young mage. Shadows haunted her with every step within the dream world. Shadows that whispered horrific things to her. Tempting her with ideas of lust and violence. They taunted her, beckoning her with accepting who she was. She wasn't even sure anymore.

Cailin just cried each night as the sun set and the moon rose, knowing that again she'd have to sleep. Her eyes were tired from forcing herself to stay awake. She did not want to dream. She did not want to see that shadow anymore.

Cailin struggled to walk with each day, the weight of her burden growing heavy every passing hour. Her eyes were heavy, dark circles forming around them. She knew that sleep would come soon and again she'd be tormented. Hallucinations might come. How could she even believe her own sleep deprived eyes? She wasn't sure she could any longer. Black specks, moving in front of her eyes faster than birds, plagued her. Flashes of light, blurred movement, and seeing things that weren't there on second glances, all taunted her. It was a hellish experience. She longed for home. For the guild, and their taunts, harmless compared to the taunts of her shadowy tormentor. For Hardstone, and the unwarranted fear they held for her.

Was it unwarranted?

Perhaps she could act out. Snap. Maybe one day she would enter someone's dream through her own will and force them to do something they couldn't control. Something terrible, like a crime. Maybe it would be something wanton, full of lust.

Cailin smirked and chuckled to herself, thinking that she could act like a succubus.

No!

She shook her head. That couldn't happen. That was the first step towards entering someone's mind intentionally. She wouldn't succumb to the temptation.

It was that damn harpy's fault. The dreams had grown worse since entering its mind. She still couldn't figure it all out. Between the ravishing of flesh, killing, and fighting amongst the other harpies, plus the other acts they did together, she wasn't sure what was the purpose of seeing. The harpy seemed like a mindless beast driven only by killing and mating. Hunger and lust.

The voices began after she opened her mind to the harpy. Magic was funny in that way. Open to it and entered. Give it an inch and it would take a foot. Magic was just as dangerous as it was useful.

Then there was something else.

What was that? Cailin thought about it. Someone was controlling the beasts. Someone was making the harpies attack settlements. Was it the shadowy figure trying to torment and tempt her?

Cailin shook her head and focused on the trail ahead. It was a long walk and one that would not be any easier thinking about dreams that were more confusing than normal. Even on the best days, even the happiest dreams could never be interpreted with any real accuracy. Cailin knew that.

So why did these dreams haunt her so much? Why did she have to figure these ones out? Cailin felt that something, someone, was entering her mind. She knew the feeling.

Was that person, that mage, responsible for her dreams and her visions? Were they causing her stress? The hallucinations had to end. One way or another, they had to end. Either with finding the source, or by her own hand, Cailin knew the hallucinations would end.

A persistent thought nagged at her.

'Is any of this real?'

DARKNESS ECHOES

Fatima, the Blackbird mage, sat in front of a stone altar. She sat cross-legged, deep in meditation. Her hands were freshly painted with the red dye that her sect of mages was known for. Spells and incantations drawn upon her slender fingers and hands. Unlike the art on her hands, which was finely crafted, her thoughts were scattered. She had hoped that within the ancient Temple of the Dark Empress Mahārāṇī she would find solace and peace.

She did not.

Fatima chose the temple for its history and power. The Dark Empress Mahārāṇī had been a dark mage during the Age of the Red Moon.

Eons before Fatima decided to meditate in her temple, the Dark Empress had ruled much of the known world with an iron fist. Her army had stormed over the land and sea, conquering many kingdoms and leaving destruction in her wake. Her only goal, conquer the world. Empress Mahārāṇī had broken free from the stifling codes of the Ancient Guild of Sorcerers. Taking with her many others who believed in her faith of using dark magic as well as any other magic, a great power grew throughout the war, taking many lives, and causing civil wars between mages and their guilds.

Finally, after nearly a hundred years of waging war upon the world and any who refused her rule, Dark Empress Mahārāṇī was betrayed. Her body was buried deep in the first temple, one of the hundreds she had built. Most legends detailed that she was buried alive in a black stone sarcophagus.

The very temple that Fatima called home.

It was there that she and the other followers heard the wails of the once great empress through the void calling out to them. Granting power and magical might. Other former mage lords were also buried in the deepest reaches of the temple, giving more dark power to the building.

The Mage Guild was built in later years to prevent dark magic from gaining followers, as it once did. Yet, many like Fatima still turned from the Mage Guild and followed their own truth.

The temple was dim, with only several candelabras lighting the chamber. Fatima focused on her own breath; her thoughts raced between visions. Incense smoke of sandalwood and amber wafted around her. Acolytes walked around her, completing chores, and tending to the incense and candles. Fatima was hearing too many voices in her thoughts. She stood from the altar and sighed.

"You all are too loud," Fatima said with a dismissive wave, leaving the room.

Fatima walked out of the chamber and down a dark hallway. She passed ancient bas reliefs of the Dark Empress' first battles from thousands of years before. She wandered the hallway, turned corners, and ventured down the stairs into the deep catacombs. Fatima knew the way well. It was a favorite place of hers. She made her way into a darkened hallway, lit only by braziers placed sparingly along the damp stone walls. She knowingly turned a couple of corners and then found herself in a short hallway, with a pentagon-shaped room at the end of the hall. Fatima walked into the room and stepped up onto the platform in the center of the room. There she faced an ancient stone sarcophagus with a large gemstone of black tourmaline chained atop of it.

She knelt in front of the tomb.

"Great grandmother, grant me vision," Fatima whispered.

At first, there was nothing, and then a soft breeze blew around Fatima.

"What is it that you seek, daughter?" a voice spoke.

Fatima sighed. "What is happening in this world? Civil wars rage over the knowledge of magic and we fall in great numbers. How can we stop this destruction?"

"Lost are you and your clan? Lost is the way of the world. Even in this darkened tomb, I can still see more than any other mage. Did they not realize the error of locking me away behind this infernal stone? I've been cursed with the knowledge they have ignored," the voice chastised.

"Your teachings led to wars and rebellions against mages. The life of a mage is to be a vessel for the balance of life in the world," Fatima countered.

"Lies. I can see through you like I could your mother," the voice taunted. *"You hate your role as a ritualistic necromancer for funerals and monks. You hate being looked at with scorn and fear for your abilities. I fought to rid the world of such notions, yet I was betrayed by my own son. A betrayal unwarranted!"*

"You committed crimes against the human, non-mage world," Fatima replied.

"I made us strong. For eons, mages have been hunted and scorned by society. I made us strong; I gave hope to the mages throughout the world. No more would we be chained by human laws! I wielded power like you could never imagine! I gave gifts of magical teachings, artifacts, and temples of knowledge. These things and places now lay forgotten by most. What a cursed thing it is. These guilds will have mages following a code of strict laws that stifles life. Those 'masters' would have you lose yourself to adhere to their limited teachings. I brought a

new world to mages, a world that did not limit power. Too many of these so-called mages only rely on one side or another for strength. They don't realize that true power comes from an openness to the whole magical world. A failure born of fear. Fear of what we are."

Fatima scoffed. "Your war led to countless deaths for the sake of using magic freely! What sort of justification is that?"

"I needed no justification. Mages then, like now, lacked foresight. What they couldn't comprehend is the magic that I felt and used. What I had at my fingertips. It was magic that others around me could wield with such skill. We were gods!"

"You deserve your cage."

"Perhaps, but you did not come here to chastise me for my victories. What is it that you seek from me?"

Fatima stood up. "Grandmother, our world is turning from magic again. Maybe your way was right then, but now we are too fragmented with no true leader. Our magic wanes. It feels weaker, but evil swarms about the world."

"Yes," the voice cackled. *"I feel it. A power so strong and unheard of for many centuries. I wonder what side I will take once freed from this cage."*

"What is it that you are feeling?" Fatima asked.

"Ahh," the voice laughed. *"Did your friend from the library not mention an ancient message?"*

"Amasis?" Fatima said under her breath. "Is it a mage?"

"Once, he was a great mage. Now he is a lich. A denizen of a great god from the days before my birth. A disciple of another magical source. He wants to cleanse this world."

"How does that help you? You wanted to make a world safe for mages, not destroy it."

The voice scoffed. *"I am a disciple of the chaos that binds us. When you learn more of the ultimate truth, then return to me and I shall teach you."*

"I'm a Blackbird! Chaos is my religion!" Fatima yelled, her voice echoing off the stone walls.

The voice laughed. *"You know nothing of the chaos that you worship! I am the Dark Empress Mahārāṇī, I was bred from chaos! You rely on what you see and those around you as a source of strength. You hold yourself back instead of pushing forward. Be gone from my shrine until you learn your true history. Until you are ready to reach your true power!"*

Fatima turned from the tomb, the Empress' laugh still echoing in her mind. She felt a warmth from the pouch on her waist. Fatima pulled a round stone from it and heard her friend's voice calling for help. She looked back at her ancestor's tomb.

"What is she not telling me?" Fatima cursed before leaving the catacombs.

* * * * *

"Through my will this world be reborn," Balt said, his mouth contorting to a ghastly shape.

He walked into the city through the outer gates, passing many of the locals. Most who saw him turned and went the other way. Some tried to ignore his hideous form. The average person would not know a lich if they ever met one. Instead, the undead mage would look like a sickly elderly person or a skeleton. Most would be wise to run from it.

He looked around the market square, his dragon familiar was flying overhead. The beast was taken from a grave mound just north of the city. An ancient beast for an ancient mage. Balt walked through, draining the life from each person he passed by. His hooded cloak wafted behind him as he strolled casually along the stone street.

The sky grew darker as the dragon's shadow blocked the sunlight. Many looked up, seeing to their horror, the dragon's massive form take shape. A roar pierced the sky, splitting eardrums. Balt's pet was putting fear into the citizens as it flew above the buildings. Flames flew out of its mouth, bellowing down to the city. Fires broke out, and panicked people tried to put them out, but dragon fire wasn't like a cooking fire. It was magical in nature, harder to control.

A terror from another world. A forgotten memory. Balt harnessed control over the beast, making it move to his whim. Balt walked down the street, his neck bent and head cocked to the right. His head twitched as if he had a crick or some pain in his neck or shoulders. Balt's grimace gave everyone pause before they even saw the dragon. It was a look of hate but of pain as well. He lumbered down the street. Each step was a chore, but with the help of his magic, he moved on toward the enormous tower in the center of the city.

Balt's eyes darted about, seeing people running, scurrying away. Any movement brought his attention. Flecks of black or white, maybe dust catching the light shining, or a spirit from a bygone world. No matter what it was, the flecks he saw caused him to look about, almost frantically. It was maddening.

People ran around him. Their pace was frantic, and their motions were disorienting to Balt. He looked to the ground; the dirt gave him a thought. Balt put his hands together, his fingertips touching so tightly that the skin whitened.

He stared at the ground, lost in something like a trance as the world, the people around him, rushed about in horror. Their screams pierced his eardrums, his mind clouded by their thoughts, their movements. Balt steadied himself and stepped into a darkened space, another world.

"Dust," Balt hissed.

In an instant, everyone around him, all those people running, the men, women, and children, faded from existence. Whatever was being held by a person's hands fell, clattering on the ground. The dust settled from where just a moment ago someone, anyone, was running around. There was nothing. It was quiet, save for the dragon roaring overhead. That noise Balt could tolerate.

* * * *

Geddoe and his group walked into the small village along the smuggler's route. It was a raining afternoon, but the village was still bustling with activity.

Amasis looked around. "This is odd," he said.

Lestrade looked at him. "What is?"

"The rain smells different," Amasis said.

Geddoe scoffed. "The rain smells like rain to me," he walked past the other two. "Come on, let's get to the inn and see if they've made it here yet."

Amasis and Lestrade followed Geddoe to the inn. They found the source of the commotion. A group of Knight of the Silver Seal were occupying the inn for their own business.

Amasis and Lestrade walked to the front desk to inquire about a room. Geddoe stayed near the door. He wasn't a mage, but he wasn't all that comfortable near the knights. Their presence usually meant a fight was going to break out. He knew that it was a possibility that the three would meet up with the knights. They would patrol the roads, and even some of the lesser-known paths, from time to time. Mostly under the guise of protecting pilgrims, but the reality was that they were hunting mages. Amasis and Lestrade had to tread carefully.

The tavern's rooms were sparsely populated. Odd for the time of year, but given the strange occurrences, it might not have been completely misunderstood. The Knights of the Silver Seal were also still roaming the lands, though in recent days they'd been silent and unseen. That did not sit well with Nash or Marcus. Each knew that the knights would be the most dangerous obstacle.

Rain poured down, filling the streets with a muddy slop. The narrow streets were empty, people escaping the heavy burst of the thunderstorm rolling in. The winds had picked up by the time that Nash and his group had arrived. The tavern looked welcoming and warm. That was the first impression, however, once Nash pushed open the wooden door, walking into the building he found the tavern less hospitable.

Across the large room was the standard of the Knights of the Silver Seal. A knot tightened in Nash's stomach. He felt it and he knew what was going to happen. He stood like a bronze statue, rain dripping from his soaked cloak, his eyes locked, unblinking, on a group of knights sitting at a table in the back of the tavern. He recognized several of the knights, from a long-ago battle that ended badly. He saw them, laughing and enjoying a few pints. Drying off from their travels in the rain. Several empty bottles were strewn on the floor and adjoining tables. They were having a good time.

"How dare they?" Nash thought to himself.

Ava followed Nash into the tavern, then Marcus, Venera, and finally Cailin. Amasis, Lestrade, and Geddoe walked down the stairs, stopping when they spotted Nash.

Ava looked to Nash, locked in a trance-like state.

"Shit," she hissed, knowing Nash's next move. She pushed Cailin to the side just as it all happened.

Nash stepped forward, his face like a stone, etched in hatred.

"You!" he said pointing to one of the knights. "I watched you murder innocents not so long ago!" Nash's voice was filled with rage.

Nash waved his hand, and the knight began to writhe in agony. The man fell from his chair, burning from within his armor. The surrounding knights stood up but Nash waved his hand again and those knights also fell to the ground in shear pain. They too burned inside their armor.

More knights rushed over but Nash was quick, engulfing them with flames. His companions watched in horror as Nash sent flames to every corner of the building. Knights burned in their armor, some rushed to remove them, but they couldn't. Their hands burning on the molten hot steel of chainmail or plate. Soon the screams echoed throughout the tavern, out into the rain-soaked street. Several tried to rush out of the building to find relief in the weather, but mage fire doesn't extinguish with water.

Patrons rushed out of the tavern, screams of fear faded as the building emptied.

Nash watched as each of the knights blistered and burned to death in front of him. Soon more men were coming to see the commotion, more than Nash wanted to deal with.

Lestrade ran up to Nash, she wanted to pull him from his trance.

"Snap out of it!" she said to him slapping his face.

Nash broke free. "Who are you?"

"Someone needing your help if you don't screw it all up," Lestrade remarked.

Shouts from street brought all the attention.

"Get ready for more," Ava said, pulling her blades.

The others armed themselves as well.

A few large men rushed into the tavern. One attacked Nash, the mage that had caused the trouble dodged a right hook and sent his own punch to the man's unguarded chin. He connected with another jab, breaking the man's nose, and then with an uppercut to the lower jaw, sending the bloodied man to the ground.

Another man rushed the group, but Ava sliced his thigh, dropping the man to one knee, before she delivered a kick to his head, knocking him unconscious.

Geddoe and Marcus handled the other two men that came running in, while Venera guarded Cailin. Amasis pulled a talisman from his pouched, speaking in a foreign language.

A darkness covered the tavern. The candles blew out and the breeze coming in from the open door stopped.

A purple light blazed, and a bright circle formed from the light. Out stepped a woman, her body covered in a black outfit and hood. She looked over to the group.

"This way, now!" she said before rushing back into the portal.

"Let's go! More are coming," Lestrade said, looking out a window.

Nash's group wasted little time following the woman into an unknown portal, but they had little choice.

On the other side the group found themselves in a ruined fortress. The rain was gone, but the cold was surrounding them, as was the dark night.

"It isn't much, but it is home," the mysterious woman said. "At least for tonight," she pulled back her hood to reveal her face. "You stick out too much, Nash."

"I should have known it was you, Fatima," Nash gasped seeing his Blackbird friend. "So that's how you disappear and appear so quickly."

"A skill from ancient books," Fatima grinned. "As is our communication that saved you," she bounced a black stone ball in her hand. "Amasis had the foresight to save your asses."

"It was nothing really," Amasis said. He looked around. "We'll need some dry branches to start a fire."

"What part of maintaining a low profile do you not get?" Fatima asked Amasis.

"Couldn't help it," Amasis answered. He glanced to Nash. "He pushed us to act."

"And who are you?" Ava asked.

Amasis turned to the assassin and gave her a wry smile.

"I'm Amasis, a mage from the Great Library of Cartogenia. This is Lestrade, a sage from the library, and Dragon Master Geddoe."

Lestrade flourished in a bow while Geddoe simply nodded his head.

"We're looking for her," Amasis said, pointing to Cailin.

Marcus and Venera stepped in front of Cailin.

"What for?" Marcus asked.

"The same thing your group wants her for," Fatima responded. "She can speak to animals, and she can flay minds."

"We know that. But what animals do they need her to chat with?" Ava asked, pointing to Geddoe's group.

Geddoe stepped up. "My friend is trapped between a dragon's mind and his own," Geddoe sat on a nearby stone block while Amasis built the fire. "We were hunting a large dragon for some elf lord. An elder dragon that is now fighting my friend for control of his mind."

"How does that happen?" Marcus asked.

"It was a sleep spell. He had to reinforce it but then the dragon was awake enough and powerful enough to fight back," Geddoe replied.

"He's a mage?" Cailin asked.

Geddoe nodded.

Cailin walked closer. "Dark marked?" she whispered.

Geddoe shook his head.

Cailin sighed. "That's the issue. Without the dark skills, he'd be vulnerable to incursions into his own head," Cailin said.

Fatima sat by the fire. "Whatever the case, your two groups need one another.

The other issue is that the elf lord has a dragon already."

Geddoe looked shocked.

Amasis nodded. "He must have bet on more than one horse. He took a blacksmith to build a great forge and his second in command awoke a lich mage. That's the second part of our mission, and we need Cailin for that part too."

Fatima sighed. "We need to work together to stop the lich from completing his plan."

"No. I have to get to my friend," Geddoe said, standing quickly.

Fatima motioned with her hand for him to calm down. "If we don't kill the lich, then your friend, along with the rest of the world, is dead. Sit and let's figure this out."

BOUND IN BONES

The group sat near a fire. No one was talking, and Cailin wrapped herself in a wool blanket to shield her from the coming frost. Nash poked at the fire with a long stick. He sighed. Blood caked his knuckles, and bruises were forming on his face.

Cailin looked at him, observing his mannerisms. She longed to understand his motives. She feared the Knights of the Silver Seal, but she didn't hold the same hatred for them that Nash seemed to.

"What happened to you, Nash?" Cailin asked.

Nash looked up to Cailin. His face was unflinching, as a stone.

"You killed those knights with little remorse. Burned them in their armor and you didn't even let them talk," Cailin continued.

"Why should I let them talk?" Nash responded.

Cailin furrowed her brow. "They had wounded among them."

"And?"

"We didn't come all this way just to kill knights," Cailin said.

"Maybe not, but I knew those knights from long ago. They had it coming," Nash answered.

"Why?" Marcus asked.

Nash looked at the older man. "We are walking into gods know what with three mages, a stone elf, and a dragon hunter. Not to mention an apostate mage, an assassin, and a wanted smuggler. I think a little protection of our secrecy is called for. Besides, what do you care, Marcus? They are bad for your business, so that's fewer to worry about."

Marcus scoffed. "It doesn't work that way. I pay off guards and knights. I grease wheels to get my way. I use contacts with other smugglers or mercenary companies. I don't kill. That is bad for business."

Ava looked at Nash. "You might as well tell them. It'll be easier going forward."

Nash spat on the ground and huffed. He stayed silent for a moment before giving in.

"We were camped south of Elith-Moor back during the War of the Salt Princes. I and a few other healers were stationed with some Knights of the Silver Seal. We had orders to siege the city. The commander wasn't thrilled with the idea of waiting, but his orders were to avoid bloodshed. Siege the city, wait, and peacefully take over. The populace wasn't to be harmed."

"It rarely goes that way," Fatima said.

Nash looked over at Fatima and shook his head. "No, it doesn't, and it didn't," he sighed. "The commander, Count Jerold of Ridgemont, some lower noble from a holding in the southwest of the Reachlands, ordered a massive assault. He used an excuse about provisions. Yes, we were starving, but we should have waited. The knights, nonetheless, followed the order and stormed the city, taking no prisoners."

"It was war," Fatima added. "We do those things in war."

"Yes, if your idea of war is death for your lord," Venera scoffed.

Fatima smirked. "All death is natural."

Nash sighed. "That's not the point. Those knights, those that I killed today, showed me the true idea of the Silver Seal. The town was an elven community that had a magical academy. The knights wanted it destroyed, and the town razed. Everyone was killed for fear of their magic. But the lie about food proved fruitless. They were far more starved than us," Nash sniffed. "The knights went mad. Blood was everywhere. Bodies ripped apart for boiling pots. Men, women, and children butchered and then thrown into makeshift pits to cook. Some didn't even wait for that. They tore into the elves' flesh without thinking. Eating the bodies where they lay."

"Fuck. How did your commander allow it?" Cailin asked.

"He was one of the first to bite into a dead elf," Nash answered.

"What of you?" Marcus asked.

Nash shook his head. "I didn't eat an elf, if that's what you're asking. I... I found a dog and ate that. After seeing all of that, I decided to leave. A couple knights tried to stop me, but they forgot I was more than a healer. I burned them, and then burned a few others that saw me. Over the years, I've run into a few more. I used to let them talk. I used to listen to their reasoning for such a slaughter. They were just following orders, they were starvation, the mages were too powerful. I've heard it all, and nothing has ever made me not kill those knights. I stopped asking. No answer will change my response."

The group sat in silence for a few moments.

"I was there too," Amasis finally said. "I saw a lot of the same things you saw."

Nash smirked. "I thought I remembered you from somewhere. You were with Jerico's company, right?"

"Yeah, I was there. After you and a few other mages split, the Knights took it upon themselves to round up the rest of us. A few were killed by the end of it. All but two of us, actually. I escaped, my partner did as well, but not before being ganged up on a few times while we were being held. Most of the female mages suffered the perversions of the knights. Those vows of celibacy didn't count with mages, I guess. She was strong, but her mind had been warped by those knights and their torture. The pain and the memories continued to torture her even weeks after we had escaped. Turns out she didn't really escape."

"What happened?" Nash asked.

Amasis grimaced. "I had gone to forage for mushrooms and berries. I came back to our camp and found her hanging from an oak tree. She decided to end it herself. A final *fuck you* to the knights."

"I'm sorry," Nash said.

"Maybe those knights would have killed us all anyway, even if you hadn't run off. Maybe they didn't need your tantrum as an excuse for revenge. All I know is that your name was the last word spoken by many of those that were killed after you left. Keep your sorry, keep your self-righteous motive for vengeance. You don't deserve it. Years ago, I would have killed you at first glance. But now, no. I gave up my hatred for you a long time ago when Lestrade showed me another way."

Lestrade gently rubbed Amasis' shoulder.

"I didn't kill those mages back then," Nash said.

"Maybe not but they died blaming you. They died cursing you, and I think that's worse in the long run," Amasis replied. "We'll finish this mission and then you can go off and do whatever the fuck you want. I'll return to the library. Both in peace knowing that for one of us, the past is in the past."

Nash nodded solemnly. "So, how did you handle all of the bad memories?"

Amasis looked at Nash. "I drink to drown my demons."

Lestrade lowered her eyes, and the others turned away.

Nash held Amasis' gaze. "I do too, but my demons can swim."

Nash turned to look at the fire, and away from Amasis' stare. Amasis turned away and found solace in Lestrade's hug.

The group left it at that. In the silence.

* * * * *

Rest didn't come easy that night for any, especially not for Cailin.

Cailin was roused from a terrible dream. She was in a place that was unknown and dark. Cailin looked around but heard only noises. She walked towards the sounds as visions began to come into view. Cages, magical and obsidian, holding large monstrous beasts. Evil animals roaring, growling, and hissing venomously. She walked through the pits and cages, taking the stares and attacks of the dream beasts. She saw someone, hooded and shadowed, standing among the terrors. It was as if the figure was controlling all of the nightmarish beasts. The now familiar shadow looked in Cailin's direction.

Was it looking at her?

Cailin felt a chill run down her spine.

"Young one, do you know what powers you possess?" the figure asked her. Its voice was masculine. "You can walk upon planes that others will never know, as can I, yet you stay stuck in a box of the guild's creation."

This was the first time that Cailin could understand what he was saying. The shadowy figure turned to walk to Cailin. It wasn't a normal walk, rather, it was labored and slow. The figure limped and struggled with each step.

"What you still have left to learn can help bring this world to its knees," the figure said. "We can bring order to the chaos. You and I."

Cailin backed away. She tried to turn, but the shadow held out a hand. Cailin was stuck in place. She couldn't say for sure, but she felt the figure's hand closing in around her throat. Cailin shook her head, pulling back, trying to break free.

"Child, stop running from what you are. They call you evil, and they fear you. Accept that and make them pay," the figure said. "It is your destiny."

"No!" Cailin yelled out, pulling herself away as much as she could.

The figure gripped tighter as Cailin recoiled back and struggled to break free. Cailin stared into the darkness under the figure's hood, seeing nothing but a void. She peered, thinking that maybe pupils were shrouded under its cover. She pushed away from the figure with all her might. Finally breaking away, Cailin fell to the ground. The shock of the fall jolted her awake, still in the ruins.

There was a terror about the dream, a realism Cailin could sense just beyond her own sight. Still, even in the darkest night, she wasn't sure she was yet awake.

Could she still be locked within a dreamscape?

She looked around the campsite, seeing her friends still in the camp. Cailin breathed a sigh of relief.

Who was that man?

Fatima stirred around the corner of a ruined rock wall. She was dressed in her black headscarf, adorned with faint geometric images, a flowing black cloak wrapped around her tunic and dark trousers. She wore sandals, muffling her steps on the wet grass.

"What bothers you, girl?" the mysterious woman asked.

Cailin looked at Fatima and sighed. "You should know. You're dark marked too, aren't you?"

"I'm not," Fatima offered a polite smile to hide her annoyance.

Cailin raised an eyebrow.

"I practice necromancy and other arts deemed dark by the guild."

"So, you raise the dead?" Cailin asked.

Fatima grinned, sitting next to Cailin. "No. I perform necessary rituals for those that have passed on based on their culture. Sometimes a cleansing of the body, or home. Other times, the actual burial or cremation with the proper blessings and a litany of spells of protection."

"Oh," Cailin responded, embarrassed by her lack of knowledge.

"I mean; I could raise someone from the dead for a short time. That's one of the many spells necromancers learn. However, that is not all that necromancy is about,"

Fatima chuckled. "The guild doesn't like to deal with death. Too close to dark magic in their mind. Therefore, those of us that study the darker arts are asked to perform the rituals associated with death and the afterlife. Nothing evil, just an unwanted part of life."

Cailin shook her head. "Death and life are separate."

"That is what the guild teaches. Sad but perhaps true in some respects," Fatima replied. "But it will still happen. The gods have seen your fate long before the creation of this world."

Cailin stood up and scoffed. "The gods have cursed me. What do I care what they think?"

"Your powers are not a curse. They are just magic," Fatima reasoned.

Cailin looked at the woman with an intense and angry stare. "What the hell does that even mean?" she said. "I've lived with this power for my whole life. Everyone around me that I've ever loved is gone and you say my powers aren't a curse because they are magic. Yes, death magic!"

Fatima stood. "Forgive me, Cailin. I may have misspoken. Yet, for someone who doesn't know more than what the guild has taught you, such as what a necromancer is, I'd be slower to judge someone's response," the hooded mage turned. "The sun will rise soon; we should be waking the others for the journey."

Cailin stood and watched as Fatima disappeared behind a broken wall.

Was the mage right? Cailin knew she was still young and learning. What had the guild failed to teach her? What did the guild not know?

She walked up to Fatima.

"It was a dream. A nightmare," Cailin said.

Fatima, whose back was turned, grabbed her satchel from the ground. She never turned to Cailin.

"Was it a recurring dream?" Fatima asked, searching through her satchel.

"No. Not this one."

"But others have been more frequent?"

Cailin sighed. "Yes."

Fatima turned to Cailin. "You are a flayer. Trained or not, it is a skill you have naturally. You walked into someone's dream."

"No," Cailin responded, shaking her head. "It was my dream."

"Perhaps it just felt like your dream."

Cailin shook her head again. "No. He, someone in the dream, spoke to me.

The man reached out to me. He grabbed me," she held her hand up to her neck, rubbing the area the shadow had grabbed her.

Fatima stepped closer and ran a finger over Cailin's throat.

"Fuck," Fatima hissed.

She rushed over to Amasis and kicked his foot, rousing the mage awake.

"What is it?" Amasis said, sleepy-eyed.

"What do you know of this lich?" Fatima growled.

"What do you mean?"

Others started to wake up at the commotion.

"What do you know of the lich? The lich we are rushing to defeat."

"I don't know much. Just some long dead, or undead, mage," Amasis replied, sitting up.

"He was dark marked," Fatima said.

"What?" Nash asked, walking over. "How can you tell?"

Fatima grabbed Cailin's wrist and pulled her close, pointing at her throat. "It did this to her in her dream. That is a power beyond mere mages and even flayers. That is a power learned only by the most skilled dark mages," she let go of Cailin. "A mage that can enter a dream and touch the dreamer is far more dangerous. Mages have studied lifetimes and never learned such skills. Even as liches. Legends only speak of a few of these mages."

"So, what are we dealing with?" Venera asked.

"A mage long dead and thought to be really dead. Not just lich dead, but 'dead-dead' to the world. I should have seen him. *She* warned me about him," Fatima grimaced. "There are but a few mages I ever knew of that had such power, and all are bound in the catacombs of Tarrega, bound by spells. All but one."

"Which one?" Amasis asked.

"Balt," Fatima hissed.

* * * * *

A gangly human, his face sunken down to the bones, eyes covered by cloth, walked into a dimly lit room. He turned toward the two elves, Marscal and Persa, surrounded by others, all of them cloaked with their faces hidden. His mouth sneered in a grimace. The room felt void of any warmth it might have held, and the darkness of the world wrapped around him.

"You have failed in a simple task," the man said. "How can I even begin to trust this endeavor to you if you can't stop a couple of humans?"

Marscal bowed to the man. "My lord, most terrible. I assure you that the humans will be dealt with soon. I assure you, my lord Balt. The harpies were just the first attempt."

"Your own arrogance caused this failure. Arrogance is a mistake that cannot be corrected," he looked down at Marscal. "Arrogance is a human trait that has tainted your kind. In the earliest days of mortals, the elves only existed as what your kind now look to as Stone Elves. They are the original beings. Pure and one with this world. From them the other races of elves sprang forth and the youngest of them all, High Elves, look down on the others. Arrogance in its most wicked form."

The old man looked at Persa. The sand elf didn't kneel or bow to the human. "You have done well to expose our weakness. Now purge it," he said in a gurgling voice.

Marscal looked up to Persa, shocked. Persa nodded and unsheathed her curved blade and quickly slid it across Marscal's neck.

Balt nodded as others came and removed Marscal's twitching and still bleeding body. "Persa, you will now lead our forces against this world. And as your reward, you'll enter the afterlife first, and all will herald you a great heroine to this world when it's reborn."

Persa smiled. "Yes, my lord Balt."

Balt sat on his throne, a stone chair adorned with skulls and candles. He removed the cloth from his eyes but instead of two orbs, there was nothing but empty sockets, skin grown over from years without his eyes.

"I was once another. I was once but a man with a strange and dark power. I devoted my life to aid mortal kind, but I was shunned and hated. My family was killed, and I was betrayed. Mortals feared me because they couldn't comprehend the power that was within me. At times, even I could not comprehend that power. I was misunderstood in that body, in that vulnerable form. But that form has withered and died. The true self was deep within my soul. I meditated before this new form was created, and from that broken, weak man was born perfection. From this throne we'll cleanse this world from the poison of all those that have corrupted it. The age of mortals will end, and beast will once again roam a peaceful world. The ancient ones will be avenged," Balt grinned. "Now we must do what must be done to end all the world's suffering. We will destroy the Far-Off Kingdom and kill the old gods."

Persa bowed. "Yes, my lord," she said before standing back up. "My lord, what of the flayer and our spy?"

Balt grinned a wicked grin that cracked at his dry and decaying lips. "I'll deal with the flayer personally. First, I must bring her out into the open," he pulled the freshly forged dagger from its sheath, admiring the patterns of the metal. "Such a fine weapon. Forged by a skilled artist, in a fire so hot and mystical that only few can ever dream of forging with it. Yes, this dagger will help me enact my revenge."

THE LOUD SILENCE OF THE DEAD

"I can't just teleport us into the city," Fatima said to Nash's suggestion. "It's warded against spells."

"How close can you get us?" Nash asked, looking at his friend. "We have little choice but to confront the mage before his plan begins."

"If he has resurrected an ancient dragon, then his plan is in full swing," Lestrade added.

"Yes, but we can still try to stop him. We should try to stop him. We must," Nash continued.

"I can get us a mile or so out. I'm not sure the exact distance, but that's about as close as I can get us," Fatima sighed.

The group gathered around the Blackbird mage and waited. Fatima pulled out an amulet with an aquamarine gemstone in the center. She recited a quiet spell, and a portal appeared before the group.

"This is it," Fatima sighed.

"No other way," Ava said.

The companions stepped through the portal, exiting out onto an open desert plain. The air was hot and dry. It stifled the group. All around the parched and stark landscape were shrub brushes and rocks. Dusty and open, but there was a darkness around them.

The sun was shaded, a dark cloud blocked the solar rays from reaching the ground. It was then that Amasis looked to the west and saw the source of the dark cloud.

"Over there, that's Tyranos!" Amasis said, his mouth agape from the sight of the burning city.

"It's still a couple miles away. By the time we get there, it could be rubble," Nash said.

"Then we best run," Marcus interjected.

"No!" Ava cautioned. "Running in this heat, and with that cloud over us, it'll be our deaths. The closer we get, the more that cloud of ash will affect us and suffocate us."

Everyone knew her words to be true. They begrudgingly walked towards the city, not sure what they'd find left alive.

* * * * *

Hatred billowed in the flames pouring from the dragon's gaping mouth. A terrifying façade of bone teeth, sharp and menacing. The flames filled the streets. Fire hot enough to melt the mud-brick buildings, capturing any of those unlucky enough inside to succumb to the terrible temperatures. The inhabitants would boil alive in their own skin before finally combusting from the heat. A truly horrific way to die. Atash Teresnak enjoyed his new life as Balt's weapon.

Balt cackled as he watched his dragon fly overhead, destroying the city. His own elven forces ran through the streets, gathering the people that they chose not to slaughter. It was only a few spared, for now.

He loved to see the terror on people's faces. Their eyes fixated on whatever horrors he conjured in front of them. Balt could feel their pain, their fear, and it fueled his monstrous notions. Their feelings were a guide for his evilness. It always had been. Even as a child, Balt could feel the hatred and fear those around him felt. Whether it was directed at him or anything else, he could feel it. Balt knew that his powers made others scared of him, and at first, it tormented him, but soon he found a use for it. He took advantage of their lack of understanding, their distrust, and their fear. Everyone feared him, and for good reason. His powers were the essence of death. That is why they all hated him. Each person he ever met, all but one.

But she no longer mattered. What was done was done, and Balt had a mission now.

The world had to end. His harpies had done their task in bringing fear to the region. The Knights of the Silver Seal could be manipulated to act against mages easily enough. The idea that they were causing the disappearances and burnt villages was a well-placed notion in the knight commander's head. The mage guild, with its backwards teachings and shunning all who were different, was still in such a disarray that Balt knew they'd provide little to no help apart from some young, easy to sway dark-marked mage. Someone like himself.

Balt smiled at his handy work. Bodies at his feet as far as his eyes could see. He used each fallen soul in his spell. It had to be right, it had to be many lives, or the spell would fail. He took out an old scroll and read to incantation aloud. His raspy voice nearly chocking in the sandy environment, but the words flowed like water in a long-dried riverbed. An orb appeared above him. It was small and black. However, as Balt continued to read, the orb grew. It grew as the souls, the essence of life from each of the fallen citizens, was pulled from their dead or dying bodies into the orb.

Balt flashed his wicked grin.

"This is only the beginning," he said after finishing his evil work.

* * * * *

Fatima walked alone through the ruins of the city of Tyranos. Nothing was left. She had some foresight in the events, to the tragedy, but it was inescapable. At least, that's what she kept telling herself. The others had moved on to the hillside, away from the smoldering ruins, away from the carnage that had been left strewn across the ground. They mostly wanted to be away from the smell. Burning flesh lingered in the nose and would be present for days. Yet, the experience would haunt you for life. Many who had smelled the aftereffects of a burning battlefield said that they could still smell the char of flesh for decades.

Fatima stood in the middle of it. Her blood boiled, but it also lusted for it. Inside she felt the agony call to her. This was part of her. Her ancestor had done far worse to far more people. Fatima knew the history, many in her family were proud of it. Others around her shunned her for her lineage. Some thought she would be the Dark Empress reincarnated.

Perhaps she could be.

She was powerful, and she felt a call to Balt's work. She wondered if other dark magic practitioners felt a similar pull. Fatima stood over the ash of a child, burned to the bone. She frowned. Her first thought was sorrowful, but another morbid thought crept in.

'What a waste of life.'

But was it? Did she even care, or was she thinking like her ancestor? Any that stood against the Dark Empress was fodder for the war machine. Any that stood against her wasn't worthy of life. A waste of breath. Fatima had heard her ancestor say as much within her stone tomb. A tomb that Fatima would visit daily as a youth and listen to the stories. Until her mother pulled her away and forbade her visits. Of course, that didn't stop her. But it made others wonder if Fatima would take up the Dark Empress' mantle, her cause, and try to finish what her ancestor started so long before.

It didn't matter, those days were gone. Magic wasn't as powerful. An odd thing to consider given that many wonders of magic happened daily, yet in the Dark Empress's days, magic was seventy times seven times stronger.

Cailin stepped closer, and Fatima turned her head slightly to regard her.

"I thought you all had gone to the hills, searching for the cult," Fatima asked, before turning back to the child's body on the ground.

Cailin walked up next to Fatima. "They did. I decided to hang back with you."

Fatima smirked. "Dangerous."

Cailin chuckled. "Will you try to hurt me? Steal my powers?"

"No," Fatima said. She turned to look at Cailin. "But Balt's followers will come for you when they feel you."

"They can feel me?" Cailin asked.

"Some can if they're strong enough," Fatima responded. "I can."

"Good thing you're on our side," Cailin smiled.

Fatima returned the smile. It was a half-smile but sincere. She felt the goodness in Cailin. The young mage might have been dark marked, but she wasn't evil, not even remotely. Fatima felt a small sense of happiness to be included on Cailin's side.

"Let's rejoin our friends," Fatima said.

A few hours later, Cailin and Fatima reached the hillside camp where the others were setting up the tents. Venera had snared a few rabbits, and one was already skinned and roasting on a spit above the campfire. Fatima and Cailin sat down with the others.

"Since we are all here now, I think it is time to consider a plan," Nash said.

"We came to investigate animal attacks, not dark wizards," Ava replied.

"The animal attacks could be related," Nash responded to his friend.

Cailin shook her head. "They aren't, not really. While they are more frequent and aggressive around this area, they are acting out based on instinct. Something is causing them to act out, yes, but it isn't intentional."

"Hmmm. So, you are saying that whatever those mages are doing, it is messing with the nature of the animals?" Marcus asked.

"I think it is deeper," Cailin added. "I think they are inadvertently messing with the natural order of all things. The entire world. I just can't figure out how, but I can feel it around us."

"Then that leaves us back with the question of what do we do," Amasis said. "Lestrade and I are here to find an ancient city. Geddoe wants your help with his friend, and the rest want to fight a lich."

"Somehow it is all connected," Fatima put in.

"I think the lich is looking for the same city," Cailin said. "If the city you are speaking of is the Far-Off Kingdom."

Amasis and Lestrade stayed silent.

"Then that seems to settle it," Nash said. "We can report back to our boss that we feel the source of the animal attacks is the upheaval in this lich's magical energy. From there, we will see if we can stop it."

Ava scoffed. "Stop a lich? I've killed many people. All were living. I have never killed someone who was already dead. That's not possible."

"It is theoretical, but there might be a way," Amasis said. "Difficult, but it's the only option we have."

"How?" Nash asked.

"We have to give it back its life," Amasis replied.

"See? Impossible. Magic doesn't create life and we can't turn someone dead into living," Ava responded.

"Technically, he is undead." Cailin corrected.

Ava shot her a mean-spirited glance.

"The Blackbirds have a way of dealing with liches," Fatima chimed in. "But it will require us getting him somewhere that we can bind him and then lock him away behind a binding stone. Black tourmaline usually works for powerful liches," she motioned the approximate size of the stone with her hands. It was large.

Nash nodded. "Then it's settled. We go after the lich and bind him behind a large stone. That should end this whole mess, and then we can go about our separate ways."

The next morning, the group packed up and made their way down to the next town, Ur Gildin.

An ancient city along a wintery coastline. Ur Gildin was the home to many elven cultures and human settlers trying to make a living along the fertile shoreline. Winter in the region was hard, but most could adapt to it if they had the courage. The land had allowed a long-forgotten civilization to rise, only to fall later through poor leadership.

Fatima conjured her portal to transport the group to the city. She could teleport them closer this time. Balt and his mages had dropped the wards protecting their horrible work. Fatima was suspicious, but the companions didn't have time for caution. Not anymore.

As the group stepped through the portal, they all knew that their fate had brought them to this moment and confrontation.

* * * * *

Balt looked about the city of Ur Gildin, burning and screaming in agony.

"Round up any survivors," Balt said to one of his acolytes.

His serving mages followed along with his orders. They gathered as many of the city's citizens and chained them up in the city square. Balt pushed aside debris from a stone pedestal taking his place at a central area in the square. His acolytes brought over a hundred survivors before him.

"You mortals feed off this land, corrupting it beyond what the false gods poisoned it," Balt's wicked grin showed his boney teeth. "I will cleanse this world from mortal poison and cure the ills given to the world from the fallen ones."

Balt raised his hands, saying a spell under his breath, and many of the people gathered in front of him began to convulse and buckle over in pain. A bright orb appeared above the square. It hummed with energy and a red light appeared around it. Suddenly, the light burst and engulfed the crowd below. Their agony grew as the orb pulled their life force from their bodies. Screams echoed around the square while Balt and his fellow mages chanted their spell, focusing their magic on orb and its pull.

What was once a peaceful city of people, rich in culture and heritage, was now laid to waste in despair and death. Many feel to the orb's power, feeling their lives draining, each painful bit by painful bit. Soon, the screaming and cries of anguish stopped. Replaced only with the laughing of the long dead Balt.

"Rejoice, my children!" Balt cackled. "Rejoice in our new powers!"

He raised his hands and a bright red beam of light erupted from his palms and soared throughout the square, hitting each of his servants in their chests.

"Feel the greatness rise within you!" Balt continued. "Feel our glory begin with these first sacrifices, but soon more will come. We will grow in might and be unstoppable!" Balt flashed his twisted evil grin. "This world will remember my misery," he whispered.

Darkness took hold of the townspeople. Their bodies twisted in their place, contorting in horrific ways by the evil magic pouring forth through Balt's portal. Even his very presence was ill and twisted. An aura of long simmering and mangled hatred brought out by the terror within his mind. Screams and cries of mercy fell on deaf ears as Balt smiled, admiring his handy work. Soulless bodies were left strewn about on the cobblestone and sanding streets.

What is it to take a soul? To sacrifice it for arcane power? It rips the very being of a person, animal, or anything from them. It is a powerful spell that only the most terrible of the evil mages could ever attempt. The soul is the life force of the being. It is part of a whole. Part of what makes them unique. In some cultures, it is also what lives on after death. It is the part that goes to the afterlife to dwell in paradise, to fight in glorious battles, to drink mead with beautiful wenches, or to live with a chosen god. It is the essence of life, but for mages like Balt, it is a source of power. Now, these poor wretches that were once people lay dead, soulless on the streets, to never enter the afterlife. For many, this is a fate worse than death.

It isn't easy to take a soul. Balt was a lich. He gave up his life many years prior, and now lives in a state that is unnatural. He uses his power to corrupt the world around him, to perform spells that would be impossible for others. Yet, it all has a price. Even the powerful Balt must give something up. The question is, does he realize it or not?

Balt eyed the city gates. His face contorted in a wicked smile, full of lust and hunger. "I feel a power coming," he said. "It is something that I've never felt before. It is incredible, but untapped," Balt sneered. "It must be our friends, finally joining us."

An elven servant stepped up next to Balt. "Shall we capture them?"

"No need," Balt replied. "They are coming to us," he looked at his dragon companion. "Atash Teresnak, go forth to our next destination and make ready yourself."

The dragon roared and flew off while Balt stood facing the city's main gate.

Balt didn't have to wait long for Nash and his companions to appear. Within the hour, they had arrived at Ur Gildin. Balt was smiling, his arms outstretched, awaiting their arrival.

"Friends, I bid thee a warm welcome," Balt taunted. "This town is lovely. Quiet and peaceful."

Balt signaled his followers, and the mass of elven and human cult members rushed to the small group. Nash pulled his sword and slashed at the first two that attached him. Amasis sent a fire spell blasting in the face of a few more cultists. Fatima had spells of her own, taking out a few more. Geddoe used his axe to chop another close by, while Marcus and Venera followed along.

It was Cailin that first noticed the strangeness of Ava's lack of action.

"Aren't you going to get involved?" Cailin asked.

The young mage had sent a few defensive spells hurtling towards some cultists.

Ava ignored her. Instead, she took pleasure at watching the scene.

"Ava? We need your help!" Nash shouted.

"What's the matter, Ava?" Cailin asked, looking at the assassin.

Ava smirked at her. "I'm not paid to kill cultists. Especially when I'm one of them."

Ava was quick. She pulled her daggers out and lunged to Cailin. Cailin's mouth hung open. She couldn't fathom the betrayal, even as Ava's blade cut across Cailin's breast, slicing her leather tunic.

"Be thankful Lord Balt wants you alive," Ava said with a wicked sneer.

Ava hurled a small blade toward Nash.

Cailin watched in horror. "Nash!" Cailin cried out.

Nash turned and, at the last second, dodged the thrown blade. He saw the assassin readying another blade. Lestrade saw it too and sent her own blade to a distracted Ava.

"Fuck!" Ava yelled, a blade piercing her forearm. She turned to Lestrade. "I'll end you, bitch!" she roared, pulling Lestrade's blade from her arm.

Lestrade rushed the assassin, her own dagger in her right hand, and she could slice Ava's arm. The assassin leapt backward and grimaced at her wound.

Ava smirked at Lestrade. "Lucky."

Lestrade spat. "No, just better than you."

Ava jumped toward Lestrade, side stepping Lestrade's block and stabbing her in the side. Lestrade winced, but she stood her ground, plunging her own blade into Ava's thigh. Lestrade's block had been a sacrificial ruse to draw the assassin close.

"This one will bleed you out," Lestrade smirked, pulling the blade from Ava's thigh with a twist.

Ava looked down and saw the gaping wound. She cursed and rushed off toward the cultists. She had to find a healer and quick.

Lestrade knelt as Cailin reached her. Cailin tried to find a potion. Amasis rushed to his friend.

"Easy," he looked at Lestrade and smiled, and then he turned to Cailin. "I got it. Help Nash, he's hurt."

Amasis chanted a healing spell to help Lestrade while Cailin and Verna tried to pull Nash out of harm's way, with Geddoe and Marcus providing cover.

"We have to get out of here," Nash panted. "There are too many of them."

"Nonsense, I've taken out more than a few," Geddoe said, gripping his bloody axe.

Fatima stood next to him. Her own dagger was bloody, as well. "I have too, but I don't think I have the strength to fight many more."

Marcus and Venera, both panting, nodded in agreement.

Just as the horde of cultists approached for the final attack, a voice boomed from behind them, halting their advance.

"My children, be still," the voice ordered.

From the crowd of cultists walk out a terrible figure of a man. He was lanky, his face was gruesome and decaying. Where muscles and flesh had once covered his boney frame, there was now nothing more than a leathering binding stretched over the joints. The skin that covered his body looked rotten and gangrene. Even his aura, like the surrounding smell, was putrid. What once was a human was now nothing more than an undead lich.

"My god!" Amasis gasped. "He really is a lich!"

"I am power," Balt sneered. "Nothing like anything you've ever witnessed before, and I grow stronger by the day."

Balt looked at Cailin. "Your friends are weak. They are broken, even now, against my children."

"We killed quite a few of your children!" Lestrade yelled defiantly.

Balt chuckled. "A handful. A teardrop compared to an ocean."

"I'll kill you!" Nash yelled.

Balt hissed, raised his hands, and sent a spell of lightning energy to everyone in the group except Cailin.

Everyone writhed in agony as the spell burned and seared their flesh, burning clothing, and melting leather.

"Stop!" Cailin cried out, pleading with the lich.

Balt let go of the spell and approached Cailin.

"I can be merciful. Many will see that. Most will never know of my plan and will only see the final hour as it comes," Balt smiled. "I will spare them of the knowledge of what is coming. Their ignorance will be bliss, as the saying goes."

Even his smile looked poisonous. His teeth, crooked and broken, betrayed whatever kindly façade he was trying to show Cailin.

"The world is sick, young one," Balt said, gently caressing Cailin's cheek. "We must cleanse it from the stain of the fallen ones, those fake gods, and their corruption. Even your friends Nash and Fatima. As unwilling as they may be, it will require their magic to bring this world a new life."

"Magic ca...can't create life," Cailin stammered.

"Not as we know of," Balt hissed. "But we can rid this world of the pain of mortality and from there, let it heal itself."

"That's genocide," Cailin protested. "It is inhumane."

Balt gripped Cailin's face tightly under her chin. "It is necessary!" he let her go with a shove. "Foolish girl. You know nothing of the powers we possess, and yet you wish to condemn me."

"I just want to stop any more death!" Cailin cried.

"We are death! We have one role in this life. It is our duty to usher in the death of this age and give the world a rebirth it truly deserves!" Balt laughed. "You and your friends will see, and you will weep when you realize your failure."

Balt turned. Raising his hands, he conjured a large portal. It swirled with magical energy in a blue-grey haze. He guided his followers through it. Before entering it himself, he turned back to Cailin.

"Last chance."

Cailin, with tears in her eyes, shook her head.

Balt scoffed and entered the portal, leaving the group alone in the dead and silent town.

* * * * *

Everyone was hiding, licking their wounds from the recent betrayal and defeat. Most of the group rested and tried to catch their breath. Others, like Fatima and Cailin, sat by a small campfire, their backs to an old stone wall, bandaging each other's wounds. Cailin's tears streamed down her cheeks, while Fatima tried to steady her.

Cailin's eyes lied to her, or that's what she was thinking. Everything looked like it was trembling, but no one else had felt any shaking. Fatima looked at her, frustrated by her young friend's uneasiness.

"I can't stop my vision from trembling," Cailin cried.

"It's the power of his magic," Fatima said, putting her hand on Cailin's. "You have to learn to steady yourself."

"It feels like the whole earth is moving," Cailin gasped.

Fatima nodded. "He is trying to scare you. He wants you to feel like you're losing your mind, and that you won't be able to stand against his power."

"Can I?"

Fatima shrugged. "I don't know, but you must try. We all have to."

The moon rose overhead. A large, pale-orange orb with a faint ring around it. Cailin looked up at the magnificent celestial body.

Cailin eased her breathing. "The moon looks so much larger tonight," she tried to grin. "If it wasn't for all of this, it would feel peaceful."

Fatima glanced up, but then back at Cailin. "That's the autumn moon. Ancient cultures used it to know it was time to gather the harvest and to celebrate the dead days."

"The dead days?" Cailin asked.

Fatima grinned. "Those are the days when the barrier between our world and the thin place is the weakest. It is then that the dead can visit loved ones, reconnect, or..." she paused. "Seek vengeance on past wrongs," Fatima sighed. "As a youth, my mother taught me to leave offerings of fruit, bread, or wine to the spirits that came to visit."

Cailin smiled at the thought of Fatima as a young girl. "Your family is magical, too?"

Fatima nodded. "We are. As far back as I can remember, at least to..."

Cailin looked at her again. "At least to what?"

"I had an ancestor that almost conquered the entire world," Fatima sighed. "They called her the Dark Empress, but she was a great grandmother many generations down the line."

"Oh."

"She's a wraith, not unlike a lich, but without a corporal form. She's locked away in the catacombs of one of her temples. My mother guards it," Fatima smiled at Cailin. "It's not all bad. She created the order I belong to."

"The Blackbirds?"

Fatima nodded. "The true name is the Order of the Night Raven, but yeah, the Blackbirds. However, the Dark Empress is what can happen when a necromancer gets too powerful and lets the spirit world infect them. I used to practice the wards against evil with my mother. Especially during these days when spirts, if they're strong enough or called upon, they can reenter our world at the point where they died. Takes a lot of power to do it, though, and with our spells warding against it, it didn't happen in our temple. Mother would always give me honey breads when we had finished. Kind of like a bonding experience for us."

It was a nice thought and Cailin appreciated hearing a bit of Fatima's history, but then it hit her. She stood up. "He needs sacrifices. He isn't powerful enough on his own, no matter how much he lies to himself. He must have help. To convert this world into nothing, he has to take more souls.

"Yeah, we figured that out already," Fatima responded.

"But that isn't the end of it. To make this world into nothing, he will have to generate a cataclysmic event. One that is bigger than anything we have witnessed in recorded history. Not since the fallen ones came to this plane," Cailin shook her head. "He isn't sacrificing lives for the old gods. Balt doesn't like the old gods, so he doesn't want their help, but he wants to kill the old gods, and to reach them, he must enter the thin place."

Fatima realized Cailin's point. She stood up and gripped Cailin's arms. "It's not the thin place he wants to enter. He'll be powerless there. He must bring them out to our world, and there is only one place where he can do that."

Cailin's eyes widened. "Nou Món," Cailin whispered. "Balt is going to the Island of the Throne!"

"Everyone, wake up!" Fatima ordered. "We know where Balt is going!"

HER SIGH

The group rushed off to the island via Fatima's magical portal, but amid their hurry, something felt off. Fatima and Amasis first noticed it. An air around them, foul but sweet. Fatima looked around, lifting her head to the smell. Then Cailin took note of the odd, unfamiliar presence.

"I feel something different," Cailin said.

Fatima turned to her, as did the others. "Something is with us."

"Balt?" Nash asked.

Cailin looked at him. "I don't think so," she shook her head.

Suddenly, a loud gust of wind swept through their camp. Each member of the group, except for Cailin, dropped to the ground, asleep.

"What the hell?" Cailin gasped just before the moon faded into darkness.

"Curris pueri fatum tuum."[2] a woman's voice spoke.

It wasn't a sweet voice, but rather a raspy, disembodied sound as if drowning in its own blood and phlegm.

---

[2] You run from your destiny, child.

Cailin looked toward the sound and stared at the woman speaking. The world around them faded into a dark haze. The woman was taller than Cailin, but not fully there, or at least the eclipsed moonlight made her look more transparent.

The woman wore large elk antlers on her head, spreading out past her shoulders. A skull covered the left half of her face, the other half was colored in a red and black design of a wheel. Her left arm was bone, but her right was marked with more red etchings and tattoos. Symbols that Cailin couldn't read. Blood dripped from her black painted fingertips.

"W... who are you?" Cailin stammered.

"I am the one that all fear but shouldn't. The one that your kind foolishly worship," the woman replied.

"Are you one of Balt's followers?"

The woman grinned. Her mouth showed half of her teeth, crackled, rotten, and discolored, while the other half was pristine teeth. She opened her mouth in a grin and gave way to a raspy hiss.

"I was here before Balt and will still be here long after he crumbles to dust," the woman replied. "I am older than the fallen. I'm even older than the beings he wishes to use. Only the Creator is older than me. We are two halves of one being. He is the father, and I am the mother."

"You're Mother Muerta, the one that the voices have been telling me about!" Cailin realized.

"That is one name for me," the ghastly woman stepped closer to Cailin. "I've been called many things over the centuries."

Bats and doves circled above them both like shadows escaping the light of the fading moon.

"These lovelies that you've been seeing in the corners of your eyes are friends of mine." Muerta said, motioning to the bats and doves.

Cailin gave a soft grin. "I've noticed them."

Cailin could also see that the antlers and the skull were a part of the woman's head.

"You're a goddess! You are the half-life of mortality and the afterlife," Cailin exclaimed. "Your face is the gentle reminder of our return to bones and ash."

She held up her right hand to Cailin's cheek. "I am nothing more than Death. The end of this world and the journey to the next. There is no need to romanticize me to bring comfort. I grow weary of it."

"Forgive me," Cailin said. She sighed. "I am a mage in your power," Cailin bowed her head.

"No, you are a human with magical skills, nothing more," Muerta replied. "I have no use for mages. What would I use a mage for when I am already powerful and invincible? Emperors bow and plead their feeble cases for immortality to me when I'm in their midst. Beggars smile and greet me with glee when I walk past. I need no magic. I just need to *be*."

"Balt is trying to defeat you. He wants to destroy the magical world."

Muerta's human side of her face smiled. "All liches try, since that is the purpose of their magical existence. All of them fail in the end. Balt is just a tool for destruction. He is on a path to his own doom and the doom of others. He has yet to see the strings that pull at him."

"How can we defeat him?" Cailin asked, her head hung low.

"That is an answer that must come from within."

Cailin was despondent.

"My mother always tried to say that these powers didn't have to be a curse, but right now I can't help but feel that she was wrong."

Muerta smiled. "She is right."

"Was," Cailin corrected. "She died years ago when I was a child, but for what it's worth, I'm not sure if she really was right."

Muerta smiled at Cailin. "All of that depends on you. But take heart, your mother watches over you and feels a great pride," Muerta said. "Accept what you are," she paused. "It is a dark world, and your future will not be easy, but accept the darkness from within and you'll walk in the light forever."

Cailin looked forlorn. "This darkness is too much. It feels too evil, and it's scary."

"Because others have taught you to fear the unknown. Others say you should be afraid of the dark, but you are born in darkness and then find light. Why is this any different?"

Muerta lightly caressed Cailin's cheek, wiping away a tear. "Trust in your heart, mind, and soul so that you will find the right way. The people of this world teach you to fear, but the world itself does not introduce fear. It is a creation of mortals to fear," Muerta waved her hand, a soft blue light appeared. "Find your path, young one. Find it, let your soul speak, and then you'll defeat Balt."

Muerta snapped her fingers, and Cailin was again in the camp among her companions, just waking up as the morning sun was beginning to rise.

Fatima looked at Cailin. "What was that? The feeling is gone."

"What do you mean?" Nash asked.

Fatima turned to him. "Whatever was here with us is gone now."

"Not gone," Cailin said. "She's never gone."

Fatima nodded knowingly. "What do we do now, then?"

Cailin looked at Fatima. "We must continue to Nou Món. It is the only way to stop Balt from doing whatever it is he wants to do with the old gods."

The others in the group accepted her answer and finished preparing to walk through Fatima's portal.

THE STOLEN CROWN

Heavy winds blew across dusty ruins, deep within a fog guarded landscape. The moonlight from a full moon lit the world around the ancient island. All around the ruins were plains of sand and dust. Nothing but sand and dust. The ruins were ancient, but vibrant. Painted walls, still brightly colored, told the story of the region. It had once been a great city. Now it was a secret reminder that power is dangerous. The once luxurious marble and granite stones were now stained black, with age and a long-forgotten horror. However, the stones held onto their great power, the magic that once emanated from the entire area. This was home to the old gods' origins on Caelus.

Balt stood in the center of the ruins, surrounded by his followers, waiting for laborers to bring up the prize. It was a gate, the way in or the way out. He needed the latter. Hours later, his men pulled a broken sarcophagus from the parched ground and broke the surrounding seal. They opened it to reveal the reason for their efforts.

Balt stood over the mummified corpse of a woman. He grimaced at her distorted face. It was a face that he had seen in a thousand dreams, nightmares of the past. He had hated her and now Balt finally had her in front of him.

"It was her! The seducer of mortals! Her lust-filled passions drove even the most pious men away from the truth. I was there, watching through the ages, and hating as Sibylla tore men from their temples and into her whore arms!" Balt yelled out in anger. "I resisted and saw the light of the truth. She was a temptress of a foul nature, but she was only a vessel of the old gods. The men of the ancient days were led astray from the true faith," Balt paused and looked at the corpse. He dropped a small amount of potion onto the mummy's chest cavity. "It is right that I heal this world from their stain. The poison that the old gods brought to us must be cleansed," he said, putting the small vial back into his robe.

The ancient dragon flew overhead, roaring as it circled. Balt glanced up at the massive beast and beckoned him down. The rotten lich smiled as the dragon touched down onto the dry and cracked ground.

"Yes, my pet, it is almost time to unleash unto this world a new terror." Balt sneered.

The cultists that followed Balt to the island stood around him. Ava was just a step behind him.

"My lord," Ava began. "Nash won't give up until he reaches us."

Balt chuckled. "It matters little. In a few moments, I'll have completed my plan and I'll open a new world for all to behold," he paused. "If only for a few moments."

The evil mage lifted his hands to the sky and began an ancient chant. A green light formed around his hands, glowing between his boney fingers. The cultists around Balt and Ava chanted alongside of him. Persa stood close by, watching the perimeter.

"If they come, I'll be ready," Persa said.

The sand elf stood with a hand on the hilt of her sword while Ava joined her at the base of the stairs leading up to the tomb.

"What's so special about this mummy?" Ava asked.

Balt grimaced. "I was shown a vision of the past once. It was many years, centuries ago. The old gods, fallen children of the Creator, came down and found wicked souls that they could tempt. Fools that succumbed to their lies. This one," Balt pointed to the mummy laying in the sarcophagus, "was the first to fall prey to their corruption."

Balt slid his right hand under the woman's leathery head and lifted it gently. "Sibylla took humankind from a race of independent souls, relying on our wits, and made us a feeble race of cowards that can't control the magic within us."

Balt dropped the mummy, letting the corpse's head land with a soft thud against the stone.

"It doesn't matter if it was anyone else, but this woman was Ymir's consort here in the mortal world. Her offspring gave rise to so many beasts and vile creatures. Her sacrifice for my cause will be more poetic than vengeful," Balt finished.

He turned to his ancient dragon steed. Balt walked over to the beast and smiled.

"Come, my beautiful friend. The hour is upon us that your destiny will be fulfilled," Balt whispered, gently caressing the dragon's jaw with his hand. He pulled the expertly honed mithril blade from the sheath on his belt. "This dagger, forged with fires hotter than the embers of Hell, will ease you into an everlasting slumber."

It would take a blade made from ancient and powerful ore, forged under the immense heat of dragon's breath, to pierce the nearly impenetrable scales of a dragon. Balt had such a blade.

It was the blade that Balt had crafted in Tsungo's specially made forge. A blade made from a magical metal, heated with dragon's fire. Balt had empowered it with dark magic, foul spells, and incantations. It was a blade with a singular purpose, taking sacrifices.

Balt slid the blade forcefully under the neck of the dragon and through the great lizard's carotid artery. The beast laid its head down on the ground while Balt collected its blood in a silver chalice. The dragon's breath slowed until it had passed on into the next world. Its body was motionless, as if in slumber. Peaceful and fulfilled.

"My lovely, I will immortalize your sacrifice in the new world that I will create for the good of all," the evil lich proclaimed.

Balt took the chalice to the sarcophagus, place it to the side and pulled his mithril blade out once more.

"The heart of the corruptor," he hissed as he plunged the blade into the mummy's leathery flesh, and cut it away, revealing a shriveled organ. "This is all that remains of her *greatness*."

Balt took the heart and the dragon's blood to an altar that had been prepared by Persa and his servants earlier. He drew a symbol with the blood using his long and boney finger. He then placed the heart he had taken from the mummy's chest and put it in the center of the symbol.

"Bring me fire!" Balt commanded.

A servant did as he was commanded, handing a torch to Balt. The lich put the flame to the heart and in an instant, it burst into a blue fire. Balt handed the torch back to the servant and smiled at his work.

He held the knife in both hands over the heart and chanted a spell.

"With this magical blade, I usher in a new world of magic, free from the wickedness that poisoned our once great earth. I harken this world back into a time long ago forgotten, but that shall be reborn. Let the masters of the old world be free!"

Balt plunged the blade into the burning heart. A bright light erupted around the altar, sending the servants reeling backward. Balt stood like a statue as the ground began to shake and the moon turned red as the flame reach new heights.

"Be free!" Balt yelled out.

A roar was heard in the mountains just past the ruins.

Balt smiled. "The first awakens to my call!"

Just as Balt was about to finish his spell, a knife flew into his hand. He dropped his blade and turned to see Lestrade readying another knife to hurl at him.

Ava was busy in a fight with Nash and Marcus at the bottom of the steps while Fatima and Venera had finished Persa off with little trouble.

Amasis and Cailin stood with Lestrade and Geddoe.

"Give it up, lich. You won't win this," Amasis said.

Balt sneered to the trio. "You don't think so? I've already begun the work to heal the earth. Did you not hear the sound of the first Primordial waking up?"

"The first what?" Amasis raised an eyebrow at hearing Balt's proclamation.

Balt chuckled. "Do you need a history lesson? I have a moment but just a brief one," Balt grinned his evil and arrogant grin.

"Eons ago, long before mortals walked this plane, beings of chaos ruled. They were the true creators of the worlds, of the universe! It was the Primordials that we owe our gratitude to for the birth of magic, for the creation of light. Night and day. Born of chaos, they gifted the world so much, but the fallen ones stole mortal-kind away with lies and corruption. It is time for me to return us to our rightful place!"

Just before Balt could take his blade and finish the spell, Amasis flung a spell of his own at the lich.

Lestrade and Geddoe rushed Balt, but the elder, nearly immortal, mage flung them both aside with a wave and a gust of air.

"Fools!" Balt cackled. "I am unstoppable!"

Cailin threw a fireball spell at Balt, but the mage felt nothing as it hit him.

"You lack conviction, girl," Balt taunted. "Let me show you."

Balt snapped his fingers and he and Cailin were taken to a dark world.

"This place," Balt spoke, his voice echoing in the darkness. "Is where we mages can come to find peace. A sanctum in the madness of the world around us."

"Why have you brought me here?" Cailin asked.

Balt smiled, but it was an unusually warmer smile than Cailin had ever seen from the lich.

"You are a mage like me. We are death mages, and it is within us to reform this universe. They have lied to us for so long. Our powers are not to be shunned, but to be respected. Yes, even feared. The old gods granted powers to those that followed them, and any remnants of the past before them were swept away and treated like demons."

Balt flex his skeletal fingers. "We had these powers before the old gods came on this plane. Long before they were cast out of their father's home. The Creator is absent. He won't rid the world of their filth because he doesn't care. If he did, then those that we love would not be harmed by the powers we possess. It is a cursed life we lead."

"Why are we cursed? Why must we have to suffer like this?" Cailin asked, tears forming in her eyes.

She thought to her mother, a kind woman that loved her dearly. Cailin blamed herself for her mother's death, draining her life a little at a time.

"We suffer because the Creator and his children care not for mortals. We suffer for the whims of beings that rather sit in some decrepit court than to answer the desperate prayers of their supposed children," Balt answered. "Magic was, no is, a gift from beings long ago imprisoned by the followers of the old gods. Fallen ones. Angels fallen from the graces of their beloved father, the creator of the entire universe. No being with more power, yet he loved mortals more than his own offspring."

Balt sighed. "Those envious angels rebelled and tried to supplant their father, but he defeated them and exiled them to our realm, to our eventual doom. They cursed us, they fought with the Primordials and locked them away. Doing so, they enslaved us, used us, and sunk us into a pit of ignorance. Yet, we finally rose against the fallen ones and shook off their oppression when they fought themselves, a war of their own making that saw many mortals die."

Balt stepped closer to Cailin. He reached out and extended a hand to her.

"Our despair, they've created it. He created it and now he ignores it. He ignores us. The universe is sick and meaningless. The Creator is a negligent father, and we are his children. The only recourse is to rid ourselves of all of it. All of those divine beings that shackle us to mortality. The Primordials, beings of unimaginable power, will be our weapons. Tools for the destruction of the immortal world that confines us. I will use them to kill the fallen ones, those professed as old gods, and then turn the Primordial beasts on the Creator himself. Destroying our chains!" Balt yelled out with a clenched fist raised in the air.

He looked down and into Cailin's eyes. He shifted and gave her an almost friendly smile.

"We shouldn't fight. We are the same, you and I. It is our birthright to fight against those that would wish us harm. It is a duty to protect the magical, natural world and those that wield such power as we do," Balt calmly spoke. "We can build such a new world together. I am powerful, but even I have limits.

The lich grinned. "You are young and needing experience. I can give you that experience. Your powers, the magic within you, is pulling your mental strings in every direction. This is something I too fought with, but I overcame. Those anxious visions, thoughts, and doubts need not trouble you any longer. It is all born from the powerful magic that you hold inside. I can help you gain more power from this world. Power that we've been denied. Come with me, child, and let's work as one."

His voice almost made Cailin give in to his temptation. She wanted to help the world accept magical beings. She knew in her heart that she wasn't evil. Her powers were difficult to control, but they didn't have to be used for nefarious purposes. Cailin felt the pull of Balt's persuasion. Maybe he was right. Maybe he could help the world heal from the old gods' corruption.

Something nagged at her, something that she couldn't comprehend. Cailin felt that Balt might have a good intention or the mages of the world, for the beasts and for nature. However, the road to Hell was paved with good intentions. Still, Cailin couldn't see any reason why he couldn't help her. She was tired. The voices in her head had been relentless. The visions were confusing. She wanted peace. Maybe he could give her that peace. She felt tears start to roll down her cheeks. She was just so exhausted from her journey and wanted it all to end.

Cailin began to reach back for Balt's hand, but a whisper spoke out.

"Child, why do you doubt your own thoughts?" the voice said in a soft voice.

Cailin wasn't sure if she was hearing it.

"Mother told you the truth of what it is in the world. Why doubt her now? Her knowledge? We've been with you as we've been with this world for eons. Balt is a lie

with his own life, extended by unnatural means, as proof. He doesn't control the magical world, it controls him. He is a pawn of the fallen ones, and he doesn't even realize it."

Cailin face changed. She knew the voice to be right. Balt wasn't in control. He was trying to gain control, but he was just a pawn for something else. Muerta had warned her that Balt was not in control. How could he help her if he wasn't even as powerful as he claimed to be?

Cailin retracted her hand.

"No," she said. "You can't control this."

Balt pulled his hand back and sneered at Cailin. "Then you will die with the rest of the fools and non-believers!" Balt yelled before taking them back to the ruins.

Amasis and Lestrade looked shocked to see the pair back amongst them.

"Why are we always left in the dark when she goes off to some magical world?" Amasis said.

Fatima and Venera joined the others. "What is going on? Why is he still alive?"

Balt looked at Fatima. "Because I am invincible!"

He casted a spell and directed it at Fatima. The necromancer started gasping for air as she levitated.

"See my power now? See what I can control?" Balt taunted Cailin.

Cailin stared at Fatima and then back to Balt.

"Let her go! I'll join you!" Cailin screamed.

A red light began to shine around her, pushing out towards the others.

"No! Too late, child!"

"Cailin, what are you doing?" Lestrade yelled out, feeling the light's warmth reach her.

A strong wind gusted around them, blowing sand, rocks, and dust all around them. Balt laughed as the life-force was draining from Fatima.

"No! Let her go!" Cailin screamed.

She felt the rage from years of scorn build up inside of her. Years of torment, from others and from herself. It wasn't just a deep-seated rage, but a feeling of immense hatred mixed in. She hated herself for her dark powers. She hated the world for its scorned of her. She hated her life. All of it boiled over within Cailin, erupting as the one person that she felt any real support or understanding from during this terrible journey was in danger.

Cailin let the emotions burst through her. From the depths of her soul and erupt out of her body. It was the only thing that she could do. Yet, she had no control over what she was doing.

There was a red aura around her, and she screamed out in a primal rage, sending the energy from her in all directions. The force of the magic propelled everyone to the ground and caused Balt to release his spell, dropping Fatima to her knees.

Balt knelt, but he was powerful enough to hold his position. Instead of falling, he conjured a portal for himself, Ava, and a few servants leaving the ruins and sending them to the mountains not far away.

Cailin panted as the force of the magic drained from her. Nash, Marcus, and the others laid on the ground, unconscious from her magical blast. Cailin was unaware of her surroundings. She wasn't in her right mind, and she wasn't even aware of her own consciousness. She could see her friends, but they were just there on the ground, blurry in her vision, yet it was only for a moment until her entire world changed.

CARRIED UPON THE WAVES

The force behind Cailin's scream sent her companions back several feet, but for the young mage, it sent her somewhere unfamiliar. At first, all she could see was a thick fog, but soon the fog faded and Cailin could begin to make out more of the environment. It looked like a normal scene. It was a tranquil place bordered by high mountains, trees, a flowing stream, and a small little shrine.

Maybe it was a house. Cailin wasn't sure. She had seen similar buildings, and some were used as both. This one looked like it had a house connected, but part of the house looked like a temple or shrine dedicated to a dragon. The area was still surrounded by a light mist. Almost as a barrier, but not one that seemed dangerous.

Cailin walked through the mist of this unfamiliar landscape. It was morning, with a dim light rising along the horizon and a crescent moon low in the sky.

"Where am I?" she said, her voice echoing softly.

"Where all mages go, should they wish it." a voice answered back. "At least those of us with the ability to reach this place."

"Who said that?" Cailin asked, looking around, trying to find the speaker.

A blue haze appeared in front of her, and a man formed out of the haze.

"I did," the man smiled.

Cailin furrowed her brow. "Who are you?"

The man bowed. "I am Liu."

Cailin smiled. "I'm Cailin." she offered a short but polite wave.

"Yes, another mage of the eternal cycle."

Cailin raised an eyebrow. "The eternal cycle?"

Liu grinned. "You are a mage that watches over life and death. You practice the essence of magic within the universe. As am I. As are we all."

Liu raised his arms and suddenly many more mages appeared behind him. They didn't seem to be physically present, but Cailin could feel their aura.

"What is this place, and who are they?" Cailin asked. Her mouth was agape from the appearance of so many unknown faces. "Am I dead?"

Liu chuckled. "No." he looked around. "We are, but you're just visiting. This is my home, and they are others like us. Though fewer have crossed this plane in many years."

The others faded away, as they wondered away from the pair.

"How did I get here?"

"You called for me, and I answered." Liu smiled.

"I called you? How? I just met you."

Liu chucked again. "Your scream was your body's way of reaching out."

"My body?"

"Your body knows when you've had enough. It is connected to your soul, and so you reached out to me for guidance." Liu sighed, but still held his smile. "Many forget that they live in the magic. The mortal world has stopped, at least time has, and so we have all the time in the world to speak. Would you like some tea? I have white jasmine." Liu said, his smile still etched on his face.

The pair walked to the small house and sat just outside the door. Liu gathered the materials he needed and set the iron pot over the small fire. After a few minutes, he took the pot and poured the hot tea into the small cups.

"This is an excellent tea." Liu said, handing a teacup to Cailin.

Cailin accepted it, sipped it. She smiled, though uneasily.

"It is good," she said. Cailin tried to offer a smile, but her confusion was still present.

Liu smiled. "When I wake up, I often say, which tea will I enjoy first?" he sipped his tea and sighed contently. "How do you begin your day?"

Cailin shook her head. "Umm, I don't know. I guess I ask myself what amazing thing will happen today."

Liu continued to smile. "That is the same thing."

Cailin grinned. "It's not though."

"Isn't it?"

"How?" Cailin asked.

"For some of us, we find the amazing in the little joys of life. For me that is in a nice cup of tea, and for you, it is something grander. Yet to each of us, it is amazing."

Cailin thought of the old mage's words and sipped her tea. She nodded, putting the cup down. "I suppose you are right. It would be amazing if the only thing I had to worry about was what tea I'd like to drink each day."

Liu nodded. "It could be. Why worry about what happens around you? It will happen whether you worry or not. Accept it and be free."

Cailin thought. It was something that she'd considered previously, though her thoughts were a bit more sinister. Letting the embrace of death take her, as she felt its call each day.

"You are still troubled?"

Cailin nodded. "Mages are fighting amongst themselves. They have no idea how to find peace with themselves and the outer world around the guilds."

Liu frowned. "They are blind to what is all around them."

"How so?"

"Magic."

Cailin shook her head. "No, we use magic. How do we not see it?"

"Not see. Live within." Liu smiled.

"We live with it. We're mages."

"Not the same thing."

Cailin looked puzzled. Liu saw Cailin's eyes shift toward the ground.

"Magic is all around us. We do not see it because we live within it. It surrounds us and flows both within and around us. When we move, it moves with us. We do not use magic; it embodies and guides us. You must trust your instincts to feel it," Liu said. "The magic is a part of you."

Cailin frowned. "I have this power in me. It hurts and causes pain to me and others. I don't want it, but I can't get rid of it. This is a burdensome magic."

"Magic is not a burden. We are gifted, some more than others, as protectors of this great power. As guides for younger mages," Liu's smile faded. "Some find it difficult to learn their magic, and that is their mistake. We do not master the magic, but instead work with it as a part of our own self. You must open your heart, mind, and soul to the magic. Only then will it flow within you harmoniously," Liu's smile returned. He sipped his tea again. "I was the first mortal to be given this gift many generations ago by the great dragon *Mó fǎ fù qīn*. He showed me the truth of magic and how it is just another part of this universe like us."

Cailin's mouth dropped. "*Mó fǎ fù qīn*?" she gasped at last. "You said your name was Liu," Cailin looked at the elder mage, pointing her finger to the man in shock. "Liu Sun, the wandering mystic of the Arcane Age?"

Liu's toothy grin gave away his merriment. "A name I haven't heard in many millennia."

"You're the first dark marked mage!"

"No. I am simply a mage of the eternal cycle," Liu responded. "I suppose you could look at me and call me a life mage if that pleases your more modern senses."

Cailin shook her head. "There is no such thing."

"Of course there is. I am one, in your modern tongue. I can create life with the surrounding magic."

Cailin looked confused. "Life mages don't exist. Only dark-marked mages like me. Death mages."

"And why do you think that?"

"It is impossible to create life from magic."

"And yet you are here telling me you are called a dark marked mage. A mage of death magic," Liu said, raising an eyebrow.

"I am. I drain life from living beings around me and they eventually die," Cailin replied.

"All things eventually die," Liu countered.

"That doesn't mean life mages exist."

"But you exist."

"Of course I do!" Cailin shouted.

Liu grinned.

"That doesn't mean anything," Cailin repeated.

Liu chuckled. "How can death exist if life isn't there to greet it as a friend?"

"No mage can grant life. It's not part of the magical world," Cailin replied.

Liu got up and took a plant from his shelf. Sitting it next to Cailin, he returned to his own seat.

"Show me your death magic."

Cailin frowned, but she did as asked, and the plant wilted and died.

Liu held out his palm, and as Cailin watched, the plant rose from the soil and back into the fullness of life.

"Life is what the magical world is all about. Who is to say you aren't a life mage?" Liu asked.

"How?"

"It is easy to kill. We are dying from the day we are born. To live; that is the hard part. To give life with the magic that surrounds us takes much more skill and patience. However, it is a skill you possess within you," Liu said. "Reach within you and unlock that knowledge."

"I don't know how," Cailin replied.

"Magic, like the surrounding universe, is the essence of life. It is a river that flows. We flow along the river. To complete your journey, you must submit to the river. Let it flow within you so that you can use that force. You cannot control the river, but you can flow with it. Submit to it and you will gain newness."

"Submit to control it?" Cailin shook her head.

"Not control. The river will do what it is meant to do. Even when we try to block it or divert it, the river will always outlast and win. It will flow over rocks, shaping them and making them smooth. The river will bend when it must, but it will flow endlessly to the sea. We can flow with it or spend our lives fighting the current. In the end, we too will end our journey as we must," Liu sighed. "Magic is harmony with the universe. When we allow it to be as it is, then magic will be pure and flow. However, if we try to control it, contain it, and constrict it with rules, then it becomes something else. Corrupted."

Cailin looked at Liu. "What about Balt? Is he corrupting it?"

Liu's smile faded again. "He has," Liu nodded. "He too came here once. I gave him tea and showed him the great power within himself. He took that lesson and created more struggle for himself. His fight is not with others, but within his own soul. Balt is a lost child looking for his own peace. He hates what he has become, but he was blind to what he could have been. Hate for his past blinded his future, and still blinds him to what he could have been."

Cailin sat quietly for a moment. She had never considered the thought that Balt or other dark marked mages were something more. Something good.

"I just don't understand the idea that someone could be a life mage when I had never seen it before today," Cailin said.

"I had never heard of such a thing as a dark mark before today," Liu chuckled. "But you are too worried about the mortal constraints. There is no life magic, death magic, or any other special type of magic. Only magic." Liu said.

He lifted his hands, circling them in the air. A green line appeared in the path of his fingertips.

"We are part of this infinite circle of life. As life begins, so too must it end, but that is part of the world." Liu touched dots along the green circle. "Magic is just another part of that cycle and one that is as simple as an uncarved block of marble or wood. It is what we create with it, but its truest form can never be changed."

"How do I master magic that can create life?" Cailin asked.

"We do not master magic. How can one master the universe?" Liu replied. He let go of his magical circle. "A summer fly cannot comprehend winter, nor can a fish comprehend the sky. Yet, they are there and a part of their own world. We too must accept that magic is much too wide to fully comprehend."

"A man can spend his entire life walking the sandy beaches looking for the perfect seashell, and never find it, but it would still be a life not wasted. For the knowledge we collect throughout our lives is much like the shells we find and collect. Not perfect, but still worth every second of our time." Liu smiled widely.

Cailin looked at Liu. "I see. I think I am beginning to understand," she gave a soft grin. "How? How can I reach this level of magic?"

Liu opened his palms to Cailin. "You can do this by doing nothing. We do, by not doing."

"What?"

"Meditate on it. Breath, think, but be open to the nothingness around you. Let the magic fill you in its own time. Only then can you enter a new state of being."

Cailin looked at Liu. "I do it by not doing it?"

"No," Liu replied. "You do by doing nothing. The river flows without trying. The river knows that to get the sea, it need only to exist."

Cailin wasn't convinced. "But to do what you can, I'd have to train for many years. Maybe then, and it isn't guaranteed, will I be able to do something like give life?"

"You are forcing it. Remember what I said earlier. Magic is merely a river, flowing from its source into the sea. We are all just riding the current. If we struggle against it or try to control the flow, we will never reach the sea. We'd only become stuck or drown. However, if we let go and flow with the current, then we will reach new places with ease," Liu closed his eyes. "Relax your mind and soon the world will open to you."

"What you're talking about is impossible," Cailin persisted. "Do by doing nothing. Magic is like a river. It's all just impossible ramblings of being trapped in the void for so long."

"I'm not in the void. I'm not behind some man-made veil. I am surrounding you and the rest of the universe. I am one within all," Liu replied. "Magic is the river of this universe that binds us all. Water like magic is soft, yet it can move a mountain... with enough time," Liu flipped his palm over gently and a ripple of blue light swirled around it. "Think not of the magic, and only of the sound of the wind, the coolness of its breeze. Focus not on the universe but instead be one within it. The emptiness it creates from a busy world. Then the magic will flow like it is meant to flow."

Cailin pondered the thought for a moment. She was confused at first, but then it hit her. She breathed deeply and closed her eyes. The world swirled around her head like a quiet storm. Images, thoughts, and all sorts of confusing visions passed by as she thought back to her life and her own world.

Soon she was seeing images that she couldn't remember. Nothing was from her own mind, but there it was. The world, history, time, and every plane of existence flew by her as she opened her mind. It pulled at her gently, not unlike the tug of a young child leading their parent down a walkway. Many of the visions showed her a history she had never even learned. Ancient mages, dragons, and battles. Triumphs, tragedies, empires rising and falling in a single breath.

Cailin saw beasts roaming the lands, ancient mortals and immortals living freely. The fallen ones coming from the heavens, and the corruption they brought. She saw the time before written history and before humans, dwarves, and even elves. Cailin looked back to a time when the Quarmi were born from the essence of the universe and even further back to the world's formation.

Suddenly, the universe went silent around Cailin. She opened her eyes and saw Liu sitting in front of her.

"I saw it all," she gasped. "Every moment that has ever been, from the beginning until now. I have always seen it. I've always felt it. Glimpses, but I thought that I was just seeing things, or my mind was going crazy. It was real. It was our past."

Liu chuckled. "Your mind has been at war with itself. You are taught to shut out certain things, but the universe, the magic, wants you to accept it. You are not crazy, but you are trying to comprehend a wider world that can offer so much. Against so many years of trying to shut it out, it looks and feels disjointed. It is not. There is much more to see, but to do that, your mind's eye must remain open to the universe. When the last eye closes..."

"We lose it all. The magic will fade," Cailin looked at her hands. "I can't let that happen. Not now that I know so much more. I can feel it. It's knowledge in my mind, the strength in my hands. I feel new."

Liu nodded; his smile gone. "Return and teach the world our craft so that it might live on," Liu stood. "One more thing."

Cailin stood as well.

"In the hills east of Jì Mò, there is an old monastery called Shuǐ Shén Miào. There in their library you'll find many treasures from my years living there. Read them and let others do the same, for that knowledge should not be lost. There is still so much that you can learn, and teach to others," Liu grinned before waving a hand at Cailin.

Instantly she was whirled back to the plane she had left her body from, entering at exactly the same moment that she had left.

"What happened?" Amasis asked, standing up. "There was a flash of light and then we all hit the ground."

"I saw it." Cailin responded, her eyes wide. "I saw all the magic."

"You saw what?" Nash asked. He was still sitting on the ground.

"All the magic, I saw it, and I can defeat Balt," Cailin replied. "Follow me!" she exclaimed as she conjured a portal to follow Balt.

GARDEN OF THE GODS

Balt and Ava were standing at a cliff overlooking a lone mountain not far in the distance. It was there that Balt was ready to complete the final step in his evil ritual.

"There is the mountain that the old god heretics used to trap the first of the Primordials, Cuauhtla," Balt hissed. "Trapped in a caged meant for the strongest of magical beings, she will be freed."

Balt walked up to the cliff and held up the heart of the sacrificial mummy. He gripped the organ, still alight with the blue magical flame, and with an angry thrust, he stabbed the heart with his mithril blade.

"Awaken, oh great bringer of chaos and order!" Balt yelled out over the howl of a freezing wind.

From the mountain, a light could be seen starting at the summit and travel down to the base. From that light, a tear in the mountain began to form. A bright crevasse deep within the center of the mountain was getting wider by the second.

"Finally, after two and a half centuries, my destiny will be fulfilled as we take the world back to its natural form," Balt smiled.

Ava turned as a sound from behind her grabbed her attention. She saw Cailin's portal forming and her former companions joining her on the cliff-side.

"We have company." Ava said.

"Dispatch them," Balt ordered without turning to regard her.

Ava cast a wicked smile and motioned to three other of Balt's servants to join her. She drew her blade and rushed into battle with Venera while the servants fought with Nash, Lestrade, and Marcus.

"I've waited for this!" Ava grinned.

"As have I," Venera sneered.

The elf jumped at Ava, but the assassin was too quick for Venera, dodging her attack. Ava countered with a slash of her deadly blade. The assassin was quick and nimble while Venera was an expert with her own curved dagger. Both women were matched in their fight.

Ava dove forward in a rush to the stone elf, but Venera expected Ava's move and slashed the assassin's blade away. It was what Ava had wanted. That was the reaction she planned on and she toyed with Venera.

Deftly, Ava stabbed Venera with her unseen blade, plunging it deep into the elf's stomach. Venera gasped as the air escaped through her lungs, and blood gurgled up and out of her mouth. She dropped to her knees in front of a smirking Ava.

"I guess I finally got my wish and got rid of the filthy stone elf," Ava spat.

Marcus and Geddoe rushed into attack Ava. A vengeance steeped in rage, but the assassin hurled her, throwing daggers at the pair, striking both in the shoulders. Each man stopped their movement, reacting to the pain. Ava strutted over them, stabbing each in the side with her daggers.

"Never trust a stone elf. They always lead you to doom. I guess you shouldn't have trusted me either, but I'm glad you did," Ava taunted.

"Bitch!" Nash yelled out, having dispatched several of the servants that had followed Balt. "We trusted you! I trusted you!"

Ava grinned sheepishly. "And that was a pretty terrible idea, but one I was happy to encourage."

Nash ran to Ava, but Balt held up a hand, magically knocking the man and his companions back each time they tried to advance.

Fatima, Lestrade, and Amasis were trying to fight off the remaining servants, nearly twenty of them, but they were struggling without Nash, Geddoe, and Marcus. The four rushed in at Fatima, cutting her along her cheek and arms. Still, she could gain the upper hand and kill her attackers with a blast of magical energy aimed at them. Lestrade was as deadly as she had ever been, slicing through three servants before finding a spear point in her thigh. It missed her femoral artery. She'd live.

Cailin watched. She looked for an opening in Balt's magical barrier. A servant rushed her, but Cailin pushed him aside with a burst of magical wind energy.

Balt took notice of the fighting, especially of Cailin's newfound use of magic. He saw his servants losing to their enemies. He grimaced, but felt confident that he was unbeatable. Still, something intrigued him about Cailin now. She felt different somehow.

"You will use your powers now?" Balt asked.

Cailin eyed him. "Only when I must."

Each of her friends were panting, but the fight was done. None were unscathed, and all wounded.

Balt stood against the backdrop of a darkened sky. Lightning cracked through the air. He laughed at the pathetic attempts of Nash and his companions. The assassin was so easy to turn, her heart hardened by darkness to the world. Ava stood next to him, smiling at her handy work in dispatching Venera and tricking her former companions.

Balt sent a burst of magical energy to Cailin and her friends, knocking them back a few feet to the ground. He laughed as they tried to get up. Balt threw another burst of energy to them again, laughing at their pain.

Marcus crawled over and knelt over his fallen friend, clutching his own bleeding side. The others huddled on the ground near the spots they fell. None were dead, except for Venera, but they were hurting badly. Cailin stood up. Her head was scratched and bleeding. Her left arm was dislocated, and she was dizzy. Still, she stood to face the evil mage.

"You won't win," Cailin said defiantly, panting.

Balt looked at her. He smirked. "Haven't I already, though? I gave you a chance to join me and you refused."

Cailin nodded. "I did, and I always will refuse you."

She took a step forward. Around her, she felt a rush of air. An unseen breeze, and a feeling of calmness. It was like a wave of warm waters gently washing over her. She could feel her strength begin to return. Cailin knew it to be the magic entering her body. She let it, opening herself to the flow. In her arm, she felt a tingling sensation and then it gently popped itself back into place. Cailin had healed herself with the magic around. No spells, no gems. Just the natural magic of the universe.

"You have no chance to defeat me," Balt laughed. "Not when I have the power of a god!"

Cailin shook her head. "No, I won't defeat you. I don't have to. You've already defeated yourself."

Balt laughed. "Fool. I am the most powerful mage in existence."

"Long ago you gave up your ability to be greater, an that was the first day of your ultimate defeat. And each day that has followed has just been one more defeat," Cailin continued.

"You are insane!" Ava shouted. "Those voices in your head have broken your mind."

Cailin shook her head. "Those voices, spirits, demons, mages long passed on, gods, whatever they might be. Real or imaginary. They guided me. They brought me to a new plane of thought. I am no longer what the world thinks of me. I'm not what the guild thinks of me. I am something else. Something greater. I am a mage, a true mage."

Ava scoffed. "You're just another dead mage."

Ava hurled her blade at Cailin. A quick and expert throw, directed at the mage's heart, but within a split second as the blade rushed to her, Cailin blew out a soft breath. The blade turned into dust as it contacted with Cailin's breath.

Ava looked stunned. She unsheathed a second blade, but Cailin waved it off just before Ava threw it. This time it materialized as water, falling harmlessly to the ground.

"Parlor tricks?" Balt sneered. "You bring tricks to fight me."

Cailin shook her head. "No. I have come to set things right in this world. It is time to restore the balance that you've sought to undo."

Balt grinned, curling his upper lip and showing his rotten teeth. "Let me show you what it is to set things right."

He took a knife from his side and in a flash, slashed it across Ava's throat. "Her blood will fuel this world's rebirth!"

Ava dropped to the ground, her blood levitating from the large wound and into Balt's palm.

Cailin watched as a red aura formed around Balt. She felt the magic swirl around him, but it felt wrong, corrupted. She recognized it. It felt sick.

"Now see true power. Nothing is stronger than magic from the blood of sacrifice!"

Cailin steadied herself.

Balt unleashed a powerful bolt of magic, but Cailin stood her ground. She raised her hand and took the brunt force of the spell. Balt sneered. He cast another spell, this one more powerful, but again, Cailin took the force and stood her ground.

"You will not defeat me!" Balt yelled, casting yet a third spell.

Cailin waved her hands in a circular motion. She cupped her palms, forming a seal around Balt's spell, trapping it within a magical vessel.

"I do not need to defeat you. You did that long ago. Or do you not remember?" Cailin said. "Sacrifice is indeed powerful, but only self-sacrifice. Murder will never defeat it," Cailin waved her hand, sending Balt's spells back to him. "I've seen the visions of what will be if your plans are fulfilled, and I can't allow that. I have been shown how to be a beacon for this world."

The force of the impact sent the lich falling back to the ground nearly ten feet away. Cailin walked over to him.

"See true power," she said.

Cailin motioned her hands in a litany of spells. Waving them around the air surrounding her. Softly, so as not to tear at the fine threads of magic that wafted about. She could feel them, their cool touch, the silky texture of the building blocks of life.

Cailin gently pulled at the invisible threads and guided them to her spell. She pointed the magic to Venera. The stone elf lay on the ground, prone and cold. The magic hovered over her. Only Cailin could make out the shape, faintly. She guided the spell toward the elf, into her chest, around the gaping knife wound. The wound closed, and color returned to Venera's skin, as did warmth. A faint heartbeat. Venera gasped with air. Life returned!

Cailin breathed. "See, Balt? Do you see what magic can do when you let it?"

Balt grimaced. "Impossible! She was dead. The assassin's blade was true."

"Yes, it was," Cailin confirmed. "As was my spell."

Nash and the others stood around Venera. "She's alive? How?" Nash said.

Marcus looked at Cailin. "She did it."

Balt got up on his knees. "You are a dark-marked mage! Like me! No magic can grant life. No mage can do that!"

"No, I am simply a mage, and we can all do it if we allow the magic to flow as it is meant to."

"Lies!" Balt said. "That ancient fool tried to tell me the same worthless tripe as he has told you. I wasn't a pawn to his weakness. You heard the voices like me, they were wicked. We must silence them with power and blood!"

"Those voices, they spoke of all of the wonders and horrors we can do," Cailin explained. "They guide us on our path, down a path of light or darkness. No matter which way we choose it will lead to the same place. Our own heart."

Cailin held out her palm. She looked at the field around her and saw a dead flower. She levitated it, bringing it to her hand. Within her hand, it sprang forth with new life.

"The magic around us creates life, and it allows death. Two parts of one life," she said. "We must flow with the magic to achieve the greatest power there is."

"And what is that?" Balt asked.

"Understanding," Cailin said with a smile. She looked to Balt and her smile faded. "You were a prisoner of time and fate. Of your own mind, even. Those voices scared and corrupted you."

Cailin touched Balt's forehead, and they were taken to another plane. It was night, it was quiet, but for both of the magical travelers it was a familiar-looking village.

"This is where your journey began over two hundred years ago," she said, motioning around her.

Cailin had transported them to another time centuries in the past. It was Balt's home village. He saw his friends and the woman he loved.

"Elsie?" the lich Balt whispered.

"It was she who made you walk this path?"

"No... no! She tried to help me," Balt stammered.

"Yet, her death at your hands turned you to this path," Cailin said.

"No, I chose this. I defeated death! My revenge for her death."

"At your hands."

Balt sneered at Cailin. "Why show me this? You heartless bitch!"

"This is when you accepted defeat. Listen," Cailin said.

They looked and saw a young Balt walking through the village. He looked tormented, gripping his hair and mumbling to himself. Elsie walked over to him. She tried to comfort him, hug him, but Balt lashed out.

"Shut up!" the young Balt yelled.

"She hates you! She wants you dead!" a voice said in a hushed tone.

"No, no, lies!"

"You must protect yourself." the voice continued.

"No! Shut up!" the young Balt yelled.

"Balt, are you alright, there?" Elsie asked. The look of love deep within her eyes.

The young Balt looked up at her, tears in his eyes. He tried to speak, but he couldn't. Suddenly, Elsie gasped for breath. Others around rushed over. They, too, gasped for air. Balt stood motionless as the crowd grew. All gasping and fighting for air. Then they wilted, their skin wrinkling and their flesh melting away. Melting until there was nothing but leathery skin and bones left.

A cackling of laughter was heard around Cailin and the lich version of Balt.

The young Balt looked terrified as others ran over. They roped him, trying to capture him, but he freed himself, running away from the village.

Cailin looked at the lich. "This was a lesson. An accident. You did not know how to live in this power."

"And you do?" Balt sneered. "You can control it?"

The pair were returned to their own time. Surrounded by Cailin's friends.

"No. But I don't have to. We don't control magic. We live within it." Cailin replied.

"No!" Balt yelled. He tried to stand, but Cailin's spell held him to the ground. "I control it!"

Cailin shook her head. "You are still so blind that you do not see the forest through the trees. You can't comprehend your place among something so great and yet you think you have control over it. You must let go of the control to be able to use it at all."

Cailin released her spell.

Balt stood. His form was disheveled and decaying.

Cailin took pity. "I will heal you."

She touched his cheek, moldy and rotten. In an instant, new skin started to form. Blood ran new, and his body looked full of health again. He shivered from the rush of blood and breath flowing inside of him. However, pain soon rushed through his limbs and down his spine.

"You bitch! What have you done to me?" Balt screamed in agony.

"I've simply given you the rebirth you've asked for," Cailin said, bowing her head. "Be aware that humans still only live eighty to hundred years on average. You've used that time, and then some, trying to obtain something that was unobtainable. Yet, take heart knowing that your life wasn't wasted. You will die with the knowledge that magic can give life. That is worth more than gold."

Balt screamed as the pain of centuries of life took hold of his body. His skin decayed again, muscles tearing from limbs, blood pouring from his pores. He tried to yell out a spell, cry for help, anything, but he was silent as his body rejected this new age. Balt's form crumpled into a heap on the broken ground.

"May you finally find peace," Cailin whispered.

Nash looked to the others. "So, he is dead?"

Lestrade nodded. "He is."

Marcus looked at the others. "And Venera is alive. A miracle."

Amasis looked at Cailin before turning back to the rest of the group. "Cailin is what, a life mage now?"

Cailin turned to regard her friends. "No such thing. Just a mage," she smiled.

Lestrade helped Marcus guide Venera up. Fatima and Geddoe walked with Nash towards Cailin. Their victory was short-lived.

"What now?" Fatima asked. "That demon that Balt conjured will seek blood. Sacrifices," she pointed to the crack within the mountain that was growing with each second.

"A monster," Geddoe said.

"An old god wanting mortal lives," Amasis responded.

Cailin shook her head. "No, something far worse. Older."

Nash and the others looked at Cailin. "What? Older and worse than an old god?" He asked.

"What can be older?" Lestrade asked.

"What can be worse?" Fatima added.

Cailin looked off to the crack that was forming on the mountain. She turned back to her friends. They were anxious, out of breath, and exhausted, but they all knew that they would have to do something.

Cailin was nervous as well, but she steadied herself.

"Before our world was created. Eons before the mortals, before the Quarmi. There was a void. Chaos ruled and from that Chaos, the beings known as Primordials were born. These beings gave the world life, and the first taste of magic," Cailin explained.

"So, that's a good thing?" Nash questioned cautiously.

Cailin shook her head. "The old gods came, cast down from the Creator, from Chaos. They were the new generation of children. Tormented, jealous, and wicked. They usurped the Primordials' positions, corrupting them as they corrupted everything," Cailin sighed. "That is Cuauhtla. Once she was the personification of birth and rapture, now she embodies hatred and impending death."

Amasis looked over to the crack. "That's just fucking great. Now we must deal with something worse than a god and happens to be the embodiment of hatred."

"How do we kill it?" Nash asked.

Cailin looked at Fatima. "Do you know any incantations for binding spirits? They'll have to be strong."

Fatima nodded.

"I know some as well," Amasis said.

"Good," Cailin nodded. "Then we can try to bind it again," she looked at Nash and Geddoe. "Get Venera and Marcus out of here. Lestrade, go with them. We will handle this, and if we survive, we'll catch up soon. If we don't, then warn the nearby towns and keep warning people until there is no one left."

Nash began to protest but Cailin cut him off.

"Go now!" She ordered.

Nash nodded and went off with the others, leaving Fatima and Amasis with Cailin.

STARING INTO THE VOID

Viri Al Sim never designed a veil for the old gods. He had built a cage. One that Balt was chipping away with each day of his existence. It wasn't a cage for the old gods, however. No, it was a cage for the Primordials. Now, with that cage breaking away, it was left to Cailin, Fatima, and Amasis to replace the chains.

Cailin stepped forward new the cliff overlooking the Dark Mountain. She turned to look at her two companions.

"Follow my lead. Say whatever spells you know, but follow my motions," Cailin directed.

Fatima and Amasis nodded.

In front of them, the mountain quaked, and boulders began to tumble. A large hand appeared from the crack, gripping the side of the mountain.

"That's an enormous hand," Fatima gasped. "Are you sure about this, Cailin?"

"No," Cailin sighed. "But as mages, it is our duty to protect this world and the flow of magic."

Cailin extended her palms. She tried to calm herself. Taking a deep breath, she began her spell. The beast within the mountain extended its second hand out, pulling itself further out of the cracked landscape.

Fatima and Amasis started to whisper their incantations. Cailin motioned with her hands, first in a downward circular movement with her palms open to the beast. A blue light appeared around the circle Cailin drew in the air. Fatima and Amasis followed Cailin's motions. Each producing lit circles, Fatima's red and Amasis' yellow. Cailin extended her arms as she spoke her spell, her fellow mages doing the same. The light trailed their hands.

The Primordial's head emerged from the mountain. A feminine creature, horns curling around its head, with bright white eyes, stared at the three mages. A hiss echoes through the mountainside. Two more hands appeared, pulling the beast further out of the mountain.

Cailin continued her spell. She brought her arms out to her sides, slowing bring them back in toward the circle. A voice spoke out from the Primordial, a broken and wretched sound.

"Ka ts'íiboltik encerrar in ka'a ti' le prisionero. Ku k'uchul le anochecer yéetel yaan k suut reinar. A tonta adoración ti'

yuumtsilo'ob mentirosos yaan a maldito final."[3]

Cailin felt the strength of the Primordial. As the beast emerged further away from the original cage, it grew in power. Winds gushed over the three mages, their powers waning from the physical stress. Each were holding their spells, their lights still lit trying to bind the monster.

"We have to hold it!" Cailin yelled.

"Jump'éel libre, le yóok'ol kaaba' yaan k báaxal. Devoraremos leti' yéetel tuláakal le mortales."[4]

Cailin inhaled, calming her breath. She felt the universe and the threads of magic swirl around her again. She mentally pulled at the threads. Around her, the binding lights glowed brighter.

Fatima and Amasis each could now see the threads. They kept their focus on their spells but around them swirled power unlike anything they had seen before.

Suddenly, they were no longer just a trio. Others materialized. Cailin looked over and saw Liu, and beside him was Viri Al Sim. Other long dead mages appeared close by. All following Cailin's lead. She turned

---

[3] Do you wish to lock me in that prison again? Nightfall comes and we will reign once again. Your foolish worship of liar gods will be your cursed end.
[4] Once free, this world will be our plaything. We will devour it and all mortals.

back to the Primordial, almost free from its cage. She directed the circles of binding magic to the Primordial. The rays of magical light wrapped around its arms and neck, dragging it backwards. The air burned and hissed from the lights power touching the beast.

Cailin grinned. *"Le yóok'ol kaaba' ma' a tia'al. Ma' le máak, ba'ale' k wáaj. Ti' le ak'abo' le conduciremos ti' le sáasilo'."*[5]

Cailin pushed the magic within, increasing the power of her binding light. The others did the same. All of their magic flowing into the spells, pushing the Primordial back into the mountain.

The beast growled, feeling the power against it. It hadn't felt such a force in eons. It howled out, yet it couldn't break free from the light that was surrounding it.

"Ma' ya'ab u k'áate'. Láak'o'ob serán libres yéetel a traeremos ak'bal na!"[6]

Cailin sneered at the defeated Primordial.

"I am hell!" Cailin yelled back.

She flourished her hands, conjuring a blackened light from both hands. She

---

[5] This world is not yours. It is no ones, but it is ours to protect. Through the darkness we will lead it towards the light.

[6] I am not the only one. Others will be free and we will bring you hell!

waved it, growing its power and then throwing it towards the Primordial. The light crashed into the monster with a great force, pushing the beast back fully into the mountain and within the new, stronger magical cage. Cailin extended her arms, her veins protruded through her skin and muscles flexed, yet, even in her exhausted and spent state, her magic was strong. The crack in the mountainside started to move and close. The Primordial howled and screamed, but they locked it in place. It was powerless as the spell pushed it deeper, back into its prison. Soon the mountainside was silent. Cailin stood, her arms locked in place.

Amasis walked up to Cailin, putting a hand on her shoulder. "It's done," he looked around. "I think."

"We were lucky. It was not at full strength given that it was still weak from its cage. Another few minutes and we wouldn't have defeated it," Cailin gasped.

She dropped her knees. Fatima rushed to her side. Amasis knelt with them.

"I'm okay, just tired," Cailin smiled.

Fatima chuckled. "I bet. That was something I never thought I'd see."

Amasis stood up. "So, who are all these people?" he said, motioning to the apparitions standing around them.

Liu smiled. "Hello, Amasis. I am Liu Sun."

"He... hello," Amasis stammered.

"I am Viri Al Sim," the other mage said, bowing.

"Yea, of course you are," Amasis said. "Yeah, hello," he looked back to Cailin. "Are we dead?"

Cailin chuckled. "No, but they are here. Better ask your questions now, they might not be here long."

"We're always here," Liu smiled. "Especially if you are inviting us for tea."

Fatima laughed, not believing her eyes. "I have a few questions... uh... Lui, sir."

"Of course," Liu said, bowing his head. "We are here to help," he said, motioning to the many mages that stood with him.

Fatima and Amasis smiled. Cailin looked out over the mountain. She sighed, knowing that they would have to prepare for the next battle.

* * * * *

"So, some mages can grant life?" Hitomi asked.

Nash nodded.

"I had never thought it possible. Not after years of being taught that magic couldn't grant life," Sabutai said. "Yet, here it is, a miracle."

Fatima stood in the corner of Sabutai's office. Hitomi had asked her to attend the debriefing.

"It's still a difficult skill to master. One that even Cailin says she is troubled with. However, she's the furthest along than any of us. Amasis is taking some of the lessons back to his temple with Lestrade. He wants to teach others some of what we learned. The threads of magic are something we all what to learn more of and experience," Fatima added.

Sabutai nodded. "That greatly interests me. I often wondered how magic worked within our world and around us. Such a simple idea, yet, without seeing it, it's hard to imagine it," he said, looking at his hand, imagining the threads.

"Amasis has a better grasp on it," Fatima said. "He'd be the better person to ask."

"Yes, they are my next stop. Once they check on Geddoe's friend. Marcus and Venera are preparing a ship now to take them back to that castle they left him in," Hitomi said. "Like you, Fatima, I plan to offer them and Geddoe a position in the guild. I hope they will also agree to join us."

Fatima grinned and nodded to Hitomi.

"They'll be excellent additions," Nash said. "If they agree."

Hitomi nodded. "I'm sure that we can work something out. They seemed receptive to communication, if nothing else."

"And Cailin said she'd return?" Sabutai asked.

Hitomi nodded to her husband. "I know you worry, but I thought it best to grant her request," she sighed. "Yet, she did say to expect her in six months or a year."

"I have contacts in the area. They will watch out for her and protect her," Fatima said.

"So, we can count the Blackbirds as allies?" Hitomi asked.

Fatima nodded. "Chaos is our religion." She shook her head. "No, not a religion, more of a faith in something deeper. Religion is a mortal construct, but this is greater than anything mortals could create. I think that years ago we forgot what or who that was. Now we can remember. We fight for mortals, though our means might be less than chivalrous than yours. It is our duty to protect magic and the order of chaos. You can rely on us for support."

Sabutai nodded. "Fair enough," he stood from his chair and looked out of his large window. "This monastery, if it still stands, it could hold long lost secrets."

"And Cailin will learn them. Yet, we should learn from this. As a guild, it isn't your job, nor is it right, to impose views or doctrines on these students. People have suffered, we've seen that proof. Cailin suffered, but now she is seeing the truth of it all," Nash said. "With any luck, she'll teach us."

Sabutai looked at Nash and grinned. "Let's hope we deserve to know those lessons."

"We better," Fatima responded. "One day, we'll probably need them."

The group looked around at each other, uneasy but certain that they would do what was needed to protect mortal kind from any danger. Mortal, god, or Primordial.

DISTANT SKIES

Cailin walked up the ancient stone steps, moss covered and smooth. The centuries of monks and mages walking the steps had weathered them down, but the stones were still sturdy. A tall wall surrounded the temple, with dragon statues at the gates. Away from the temple were the mountains of Jì Mò. High peaks, covered in trees with waterfalls flowing into calm streams, and leading to a tranquil river. Clouds wafted peacefully around the mountainside where villages dotted the land.

Cailin loved walking along the grounds whenever she wasn't deep in study. The monks of the temple were usually silent, giving Cailin peace while she rested and healed. The last battle with the Primordial had drained her more than she had realized. The monks at Shuǐ Shén Miào were aware of how to heal the drain of heavy magical use.

Once recovered enough to get out of bed, the monks welcomed Cailin to their home. Most wore blue or green robes, walked with staffs and rope beads. Many spent their days in meditation, practicing their magic, and doing chores. Cailin adapted to the lifestyle quickly. It was a steady routine, but it was liberating.

Upon her entrance, Cailin had been taken under the wing of an elder monk and mage named Hameen. He was a friendly, open man of nearly eighty. Still energetic and thoughtful, always full of wisdom. It was with Hameen that Cailin began to learn her true path.

"The works, scrolls and other delicate documents require a special touch," Hameen said, walking into the library alongside Cailin. "When you are comfortable with that technique, then you will be able to read them."

"They aren't forbidden from me?"

Hameen smiled. "No, but you must be able to touch them without touching them to open the scrolls and move the pages."

He stopped and extended his palm out to an enormous book, bringing it to the table next to him. "A flower is a great start, but heavier objects require more practice. Without the physical touch of mortals, we can ensure their longevity."

"Can't we transcribe them?" Cailin asked.

"We can," Hameen answered. "But it would take many years." He waved his hand at a nearby door. It opened, revealing a large room filled to the top with shelves of books, scrolls, and ancient parchments. "This is the library of Liu Sun and other masters from before recorded time until the previous age."

Cailin gasped and marveled. "It is amazing. So many texts."

"All detailing each master's journey and life. Sometimes, more than one life," Hameen said, walking into the library. "One day, I hope you write your own story to add to this collection."

Cailin followed behind. "The guild will want to read these."

"I can only hope that they would take these works with wisdom and as they are meant for guidance," Hameen replied.

"I think Sabutai would."

Hameen smiled softly. "From what you've told me of your former teacher, he seems like a good man and is open to change," he sighed. "The guild for many years has been more like a religion. Mandating rules for the sake of control rather than learning. Magic is not about controlling or manipulation, but an essence of life," he stiffened. "The guild, like other religions, is a mortal creation. It is imperfect, trying to perfect something that doesn't need to be perfect. It is manipulation of the natural world. While it is good in ideals, it is corrupted and turned by mortal whims."

"We can teach them a new way."

"Let us hope. However, people more often than not get in their own way," Hameen responded.

"They will have to learn if they want to stand a chance to defend this world," Cailin said.

"I fear for this world. That Primordial you defeated was just one of many, all caged with ancient chains that are crumbling. Without you there or others who have learned how, we maybe at a disadvantage."

Cailin nodded. "Then I'll have to teach others and be ready to do what must be done."

Hameen nodded. "Then let us begin."

* * * * *

Deep within the catacombs of one of the few remaining temples devoted to the Dark Empress, a strange sound was heard echoing off the walls. A loud clang of metal snapping, and the echoing sound of a metal chain falling onto the cold stone floor.

A large stone, a mystical gem, was latched atop the empress' tomb. A seal to keep her imprisoned in her sarcophagus. Once four chains held the stone in place. Now there were only three chains holding the stone. After thousands of years, the chains were corroding and showing signs of wear.

Soon, the Dark Empress' patience was going to be rewarded.

* * * * *

In an ancient and ruined castle, Verix opened his eyes. Ablaze with light and knowledge. Still in the bed that Geddoe had left him in, but abandoned by the other hunters that Geddoe had assigned to watch over him until his return.

"They are coming," he said, before getting out of the bed.

ABOUT THE AUTHOR

Joseph S. Samaniego is a historian from North Carolina specializing in medieval European history. Joseph has received his Master of Arts in History from Southern New Hampshire University and plans to continue at some point to earn a PhD. When not spending time with his family, Joseph spends time reading, writing and playing video games.